The Doc's
Christmas Miracle

by

S. A. Stolin

Cover Art by *Tina Lynn Stout*

The Wild Rose Press, Inc.
PO Box 708
Adams Basin, NY 14410-0708
Visit us at www.thewildrosepress.com

Publishing History
First Edition, 2025
Trade Paperback ISBN 978-1-5092-6281-6
Digital ISBN 978-1-5092-6282-3

Published in the United States of America

Dedication

For David

Acknowledgement

Thanks to my terrific editor Judi Mobley and my friend and editor Dee Tenorio

Chapter One

Dr. Mark Moore couldn't believe what he was doing. Sam Heard Clinic. Six hundred miles north of San Francisco and miles from his old life. Seated in the Sierra Nevada mountains, with a gorgeous lake, it was the perfect place for the peace and quiet he needed and desired. A new start. And hope for his memory machine. A second chance to prove what he could do for those suffering with dementia. After ten years of perfecting it, he'd only been met with chiding and jealousy.

Now, here he was, self-exiled to the small town of Crescent Hill. At Christmas time. He took in a deep breath. Soft snow flakes tapped his cheeks as he revved his motorcycle up a short hill. On either side trees stood stripped of foliage, their limbs stark against the afternoon winter sky. Suddenly, as the bike swerved to avoid a charred piece of timber, he noticed a burned-out building ahead that looked out of place in the serene landscape, but he wasn't about to let the eyesore of a heap of burned boards dampen the thrill of change. He rode around the scorched wood and continued up the icy road until he saw it: Sam Heard Clinic; its name etched into the stone above the majestic building's double glass doors. Its sturdy granite walls thick and gray. Icicles clung to the eaves of an overhanging roof.

Mounds of snow half-buried the front steps. Green wreaths with red felt bows hung on each door, and a long, stone bench pushed up against the clinic wall was the only outdoor furniture in the wrap-around porch.

Mark pulled into an empty parking space in front of the entrance and straddled the bike. He wanted to savor one last moment of cold frost biting at his cheeks. All of a sudden, his quiet moment was shattered by a blood-curdling scream from inside the clinic. The bellowing cry of an elderly man. Mark leapt off the bike, threw his helmet into the backseat, and took the steps to the entrance two at a time. He yanked open the front doors—

"—Let go of me!"

Mark snapped into caregiver mode. His pulse quickened as his gaze immediately locked onto a white-haired elderly man running down the corridor directly at him, or more likely toward the entrance, his hospital gown open and flapping behind him. A young woman, perhaps in her late twenties, a vision of an angel in a white jacket, chased him, her stethoscope bobbing off her chest. Long, shiny black hair flowed behind her, and her huge dark eyes widened as she tried to catch up to him. Clearly one of the staff. Perhaps a resident.

"Mr. Johnson, calm down. You can't leave. Please, just let me help you."

The older gentleman made one last dash, bumping into Mark, and knocking them both into the floor to ceiling Christmas tree standing in a corner. The tree swayed, ornaments tinkled, bobbing from being jostled, but didn't topple.

"Code red in reception!" A frantic call came over the intercom.

The old man looked achingly into Mark's eyes. "Save me. They're out to get me."

"Mr. Johnson." Mark held him gently, staring at

him, unsure of what he'd stepped into.

The old fellow shot a look behind him and then back at Mark. "You must let me go! I don't know where I am!"

"Mr. Johnson. It's all right. We're here to help. The young female doctor caught up with him and struggled to pull him from Mark's grasp.

"Leave me alone!" He pushed her away, his face contorting in panic.

The doctor pulled a syringe out of her jacket pocket, but as she stepped in to administer the shot, the old gentleman jerked.

Mark lurched forward and grabbed the syringe as it fell from her grasp, and injected the elderly man in his exposed arm.

The doctor stepped forward. "Oh, please tell me you work here."

"Actually, I'm your new hire, Dr. Mark Moore, the Alzheimer's researcher. I would shake your hand, but…" He nodded at the now calmer gentleman in his arms.

"Well you certainly know how to make an entrance." Her tone indicated it wasn't a good one.

Mark shifted Mr. Johnson to his side, allowing the man to stand somewhat on his own.

A middle-aged lady dressed in a mid-length sweater dress, opened a side door behind the reception desk, and lifted a partition in the counter. "That medicine usually calms him right down," she said, stepping into the hall.

"I'm Beverly McFarland, the receptionist, handy-woman, go-getter, whatever you need." Mark nodded at her grateful for the welcoming gesture that he hadn't gotten from the young doctor. "Herman…I mean Dr. Dennis, mentioned a new hire was arriving. Welcome."

A young, blonde nurse and a gangly male orderly

pushing a gurney rushed down the hallway out of breath and stopped in front of them.

"Oh, my goodness." The nurse clutched a hand to her heart and looked at Mark. "Hello, thank you. Whoever you are! I'm Emily Saunders, one of the nurses. Thank you so much."

"Let me help you get him up there," Mark said as the three gently lifted Mr. Johnson onto the gurney.

"Rodney Allen," the orderly nodded to Mark as he stepped back and watched them strap Mr. Johnson in.

"I think he might be having sundown syndrome," Mark offered, trying to ease the obvious tension. "When it gets late, he probably gets confused."

The female doctor stared at him, obviously unimpressed and agitated. "Yes. We are all well aware of what sundown syndrome is. Many dementia patients have that problem." Her expression remained blank. "And in this particular case, Mr. Johnson's dementia seemed to trigger sudden confusion. We're not even sure just yet that he has Alzheimer's. Although it is the most common kind of dementia. And he's in an unfamiliar environment. He's only been with us a little less than two weeks."

"Perhaps we can get him into a private room?"

"No, he has his own room down the hall," the doctor said.

"He's the kind of patient my machine was designed to help," Mark answered, but when she didn't respond he added, "Today was supposed to be my first day, Dr…." His eyes dropped down to her jacket where he hoped to see a name tag, but there was none. "And Dr. Dennis promised…"

"Dr. Dennis is dead." She blurted out the words so

unemotionally that for a moment Mark wasn't sure he'd heard her correctly.

He glanced around unable to form words. *Dead? How?* Before he could gather himself to ask, Beverly slipped a hand into the pocket of her crisply ironed shirtdress and drew out a neatly folded handkerchief. Her lips trembled. She lifted her glasses onto her forehead and dabbed at her eyes, then tucked the handkerchief away quickly—as if erasing the moment. "I'm so sorry, Dr. Moore. You see, Dr. Dennis was killed in a boating accident yesterday afternoon on Lake Merced. His two teen sons were in the boat, but unhurt. And a week before Christmas, too. It's been horrible."

For a moment she studied them both. "Sue, I don't think Dr. Moore knew any of this, am I right?" She reached for Mark's hand and held it tightly in both of hers for a moment too long, as if he were a beacon of strength for her.

She shook her head. "It's an unbelievable tragedy and I don't think any of us have been able to process it yet."

"I-I…just spoke to him yesterday morning," Mark babbled, then cleared his throat. "He was so enthusiastic about my machine." He stood in stunned silence. The news of Dr. Dennis's death felt surreal. He glanced at Beverly, and a wave of sympathy washed over him. Poor woman. He turned to Susan, her eyes brimming but steady, and reached out instinctively, brushing his hand against her arm.

"I'm very sorry," he murmured. "Dr. Dennis…believed in me. I don't even know what happens to the machine now. I don't mean to sound unsympathetic. I'm just taken off guard."

"Well, we all heard you were coming. Dr. Moore, is it?" The young woman looked directly into his face with a sense of detachment. "You're the one with the magic memory machine."

Mark felt a pang at the mention of his machine. "Yes." He avoided her stare. "But the machine isn't magic, and please, call me Mark." He waited a moment, then as the tension crackled between him and Susan, he blurted, "And what is your name...I mean other than 'Susan.' "

She pulled aside her jacket revealing her identification card pinned to a pocket. "Susan Pace, M.D., Psychiatry."

"Oh, well, hello. Nice to meet you." He turned his head toward Beverly. She retreated behind the reception counter and busied herself with paperwork, her eyes fixed intently on a task.

"Where's Dr. Pace?" Mr. Johnson yelled out at no one in particular. His slurred words were barely intelligible, his wide eyes searching Mark's face. His head lolled back and forth for a moment. Still groggy, and struggling against the straps, his eyes open and his gaze darting from face to face, he tried to sit up, but flopped back again.

"I'm right here, Ezra." Susan stepped forward.

"I don't belong here!"

"You're fine, Ezra." She assured him putting a gentle hand on his shoulder.

Mr. Johnson swiped it off. "I'm not fine, Susan. Everything's blurry." He shot a look to Mark. "What did you give me, young man?"

Mark looked querulously at Susan. She answered for him. "Ezra, it's the same light tranquilizer we always give you when you get excited. Remember? To help you sleep."

Mark reached for Mr. Johnson's wrist. His pulse was slowing.

"Sir, my name's Mark. And let me assure you, you're in a nice, safe clinic." He watched Mr. Johnson for a moment. "Feeling a little better?"

"I feel like I was kicked by a mule—a big one." His eyes closed, and he settled into sleep.

Emily, the nurse, turned once more to Mark. "Again, thank you, Doctor. And welcome."

"We'll move him to his room now," Rodney said.

Mark immediately stepped forward. "Glad to help, Emily. May I call you Emily?"

"Oh, yes, Doctor."

Mark cast a sideways glance at Susan just long enough for her to catch it. Victory, mild but satisfying. Then he leaned his arms on the reception counter as Susan brushed a strand of black hair from her forehead, her deep eyes sharp and assessing.

Mark chuckled. "Well, that's quite a first day. By the way, I'm very glad to meet you, doctor. Dr. Dennis mentioned you—in a very positive light." He held out his hand, but when she didn't respond, he dropped it to his side.

The truth was Mark just couldn't shake the thought: *Geez, how could someone so beautiful be so cold?* There was an air of authority about her that demanded instant respect. It was true, Herman Dennis, Chief of the Alzheimer's Service, had mentioned her briefly when offering Mark the position at the clinic—but nothing had prepared him for the impact of seeing her in person. Her beauty was startling, made all the more disarming by the edge in her gaze.

Susan jolted him out of his reverie. "By the way, where is this miracle machine? I trust it didn't get lost on the way up here?" Her voice dripped with disdain. His stomach tightened at her judgment and thinly veiled skepticism.

He cleared his throat. "Dr. Dennis told me he would keep it in the auditorium. I'm pretty sure it arrived— before I did."

"Hmm. Well, I'm most interested in seeing it. Did Dr. Dennis mention to you that I, too, work with Alzheimer's patients, but I use a more holistic approach. I use talk therapy and to tell you the truth, Dr. Moore, I think talk therapy combined with music therapy are really the keys to opening up memories and retaining them. I've never believed in machines to do what human contact can do."

Mark wasn't sure how to answer her, except to defend his work, and he was getting tired of doing so. He'd hoped coming here would allow him to demonstrate what the machine could actually do before it was shot down—yet again. "The machine is a new approach to memory retrieval, Dr. Pace, especially in Alzheimer's patients. This machine—" pride swelled inside him "—replenishes a naturally occurring enzyme that is often depleted in older patients."

Susan uncrossed her arms, but her posture remained as stick straight as an army sergeant, dripping with challenge and skepticism. Mark straightened, too, determined not to be rattled—or by allowing the unexpected surge of attraction to her interfere with his position here. In a feeble attempt to keep his expression neutral, he said, "And I'd like you to call me Mark."

She averted her eyes. Nope. Nothing it seemed would loosen her coldness, and she clearly wasn't buying his attempt at a truce.

"I'm aware of your research, but you see, Doctor, my approach has been quite successful for five years. I'm not sure why Doctor Dennis needed someone else."

Mark stiffened. He had to admit to himself, he'd wondered the same thing, after the negative publicity the machine had received. "I'm aware that traditional therapy has its place." He so wanted to call her 'Susan' but knew it was too soon. "Dr. Pace, my machine—"

"Is controversial," she finished his sentence, a sharp edge to her words. "We've heard the stories."

Ah, there it was. Anger flared in his chest, but he forced it down. Fighting with a colleague right now wouldn't help anyone.

"I'm not here to cause trouble." He touched her arm.

She started at his touch—but didn't pull away.

He reluctantly let his hand drop.

She gave a small nod, her voice low. "He believed in all of us."

"Dr. Dennis was so enthusiastic about my machine," Mark offered. "He reassured me since this was the only clinic around that dealt exclusively with dementia, the machine could be an asset. I hope I can still make us all proud."

Susan's response cut to the quick. "Well, my question isn't what happens to your machine, Dr. Moore. My question is: what happens when the machine doesn't help? When one of our patients gets hurt because of your 'brilliant invention'?"

Her words smarted, but Mark didn't flinch, knowing she must have read about Mr. Rothberg's death—in San

Francisco. It'd made headlines for a week.

"I would never let what happened in San Francisco ever happen again. The machine got a rotten reception because no one charted the patient's already existing heart trouble. He died of stress. Hopefully, unlike that hospital, your files have accurate histories of your patients."

Susan studied him for a moment longer, then sighed. "We'll see, Dr. Moore, we'll soon see."

She handed Beverly her white jacket and pulled her coat off the free-standing coat rack. Without a look back, she opened the front door and stepped into the freezing air. Mark stood at the reception desk and watched her disappear down a small embankment.

****

Mark exhaled slowly, trying to keep his composure. Beverly leaned across the counter.

"Come on. Let's grab some donuts in the breakroom—and I'll fill you in on all the gossip."

Did his nerves show that much?

She guided him past patient rooms to a small breakroom where a large, pink box of untouched donuts sat in the middle of a table that was surrounded by ladder chairs.

"Well, what's it gonna be, Dr. Moore?" She pulled out a glazed donut and took a bite. "Oh, good, they're fresh." She looked up at him and gave him a wan smile. "Glazed or plain?"

"Glazed, thank you."

She handed him one with a napkin, then took another bite into hers. "Grab some coffee." She pointed to the coffee maker and some cups sitting on a long counter, then sat heavily in one of the chairs, her attention fully on her donut.

Mark poured a cup, and sat opposite her. How the hell did it all come to this? He was thirty-two and had been a star pupil and then researcher in San Francisco, but it had all gone south when the news media blamed his machine for causing the death of Mr. Ira Rothberg. The coroner and even the staff at the hospital itself said the machine was not at fault, but the next day the headlines in the *Times* were devastating: "Doctor's Magic Memory Machine Kills Patient."

It was a lie, but they had to blame someone, and he was chided and shunned by the very medical group that had been so enthusiastic when he'd first presented his research. He had one choice: leave, and he did as soon as Dr. Dennis had called him, saying he'd read about Mark's work in a little known medical journal and was curious about how the machine worked. Dr. Dennis essentially offered him a second chance and Mark had jumped at it. It also got him far away from Angela.

He took a long sip of coffee, then abruptly stood, moved across the room, and poured the bitter liquid down the sink.

"That bad, eh?" Beverly laughed.

Mark turned back, having forgotten that the ward clerk was even there. "Not at all. A bad memory."

"We've all had those, Doctor." She stood and wiped her face. "Listen, it's pandemonium around here right now. Why don't you go home or wherever Dr. Dennis set you up and get some rest? Come back tomorrow all fresh and ready to start anew."

He had to admit, that sounded perfect. He needed to get out of there, regroup. This had been a heck of a way to introduce himself to the staff. If he didn't know better, he'd swear his machine was cursed. He shook his head, clearing away the melancholy. Maybe tomorrow this place would have better vibes.

"Looks like it's going to be an uphill battle here, too," he murmured, eyes downcast, his voice more to himself than anyone else.

Beverly rose slowly. "Don't plug in to Dr. Pace's negativity right now, Mark. She's got a lot going on."

As he moved to the door, he lifted his head, grateful and surprised she'd called him by his first name. "Good to know. I'm glad it's not all me and my machine."

"No—" Beverly straightened, pushing the chair back. "—Believe me, it's not. Get a good night's sleep. See you tomorrow."

Once outside, he took in a deep breath of fresh air and jumped on the motorcycle. He looked up just long enough to see Beverly, coffee cup in hand, waving to him through the glass front windows. He waved back, and took off down the hill. His past may have followed him to Sam Heard Clinic, but now more than ever he had something to prove—not just to himself, but to everyone who doubted him.

****

Mark followed a winding path to his new lodgings, and once outside the log-cabin, he slumped releasing the tension in his body. He was more worn out than he'd thought.

A soft blue haze settled over the distant horizon, obscuring the small town below except for the random blaze of festive holiday lights. Christmas up here would be beautiful—beautiful if not for the uncertainty of his new beginning. He pulled off the over-night suitcase he'd strapped to the back of his motorcycle, and turned his attention to the cabin.

It was a perfect retreat nestled among the snow-dusted pines—a sanctuary of quiet beauty. Snow shimmered on the rough-hewn logs from which it was built, and flat, wood steps led up to a sturdy, inviting wooden door. He pulled out the key Dr. Dennis had sent him in a letter, weeks before he'd called to confirm his appointment, and shoved it into the lock, but the door opened on its own. He shrugged and stepped into a beautifully furnished, but chilly living room. He pushed the door, but it didn't close. Oh, boy. He looked around and saw a fully stocked bookcase. He grabbed three large tomes of medical books, shoved the door closed, and laid the books on the floor in front of it. He'd be safe for the night, hopefully. Tomorrow he'd look for a hardware store in town; he was sure he could fix the damn thing himself with a screw and a hammer.

His turned back and his gaze fell on the solid stone fireplace next to a floor to ceiling bay window which looked out on the lake and farther down, the quaint city. It made him shiver. This might be paradise, but he still could use a little heat. He didn't have the strength to build a fire, but at least there was a wrought iron gate-style holder, elegant and sturdy like something pulled from an old manor house, that held a poker, tongs, a shovel and a brush. A few wood logs lay in the hearth.

He heaved in a long breath, his chest expanding with the effort, then exhaled slowly. A nine-foot couch stretched across the opposite wall. He fell onto it and adjusted three overstuffed pillows under his head. A glass coffee table sat in front of the couch, with a richly designed Native American throw rug on the carpet beneath it. Two chairs with the same brown velvet upholstering sat on either side. A gorgeous bear pelt hung from a wall separating the kitchen from a circular staircase leading up to a loft.

He got up and climbed the steps until he came eye-level with the small room. A king-sized bed dominated the space, promising deep rest. Ah, a man cave par excellence.

Making his way down the stairs, his stomach growled, and he strode into the kitchen. This cabin was going to be home for as long as it took him to redeem himself. He found the refrigerator fully stocked. A plastic bag of mozzarella cheese sat on the first shelf, and he opened it and bit into a piece, then traipsed back to the couch, and collapsed fully dressed, this time not to get up again for anybody or anything.

He closed his eyes, but he couldn't sleep. The unwanted vision of Susan took over. His mind was consumed with the thought of her huge black eyes, her perfect skin, and her small body. She was going to be a problem. Her skepticism was clear, and Mark wasn't sure if he could ever win her over. True she didn't seem to be conniving like Angela, but she was secretive. She looked like she had the same strength as his former fiancée, and he could see Angela's determination in Susan. He reminded himself Angela had been a Jekyll and Hyde, convincing him he could never trust a woman again.

A thick, wool blanket lay neatly folded at the foot of the couch and he kicked off his boots and pulled it up to his chest, covering him in warmth. He laid an arm over his eyes, but sleep still eluded him. Instead, all he could see were the small dimples at the corners of Susan's mouth crinkling as she dripped with disdain over his machine.

He wriggled and turned on his side, then leaned on his elbows. Her antagonism rattled him or was it the unexpected surge of attraction coursing through him, he couldn't tell which and he didn't want either. He stared at the bay window. A layer of frost was piling up on the ledge outside. A breeze drifting in underneath the window carried the scent of pine. At last, a white Christmas. Wonderful.

He pulled the blanket around him and snuggled in.

How the hell was he supposed to plan the work ahead? Maybe if he repeated a mantra he could finally drift off to sleep and it would all come to him plain and simple in the morning. *Focus on the patients. Prove the machine works. Everything else will fall into place.*

It seemed to be working. His mind shifted to the clinic. It was small, but it had potential. He'd try a few patients on his machine first and see how they responded. Then ask the staff what they thought. If they were as open-minded as Dr. Dennis had been, there really would be hope for his machine at Sam Heard.

And what would Susan Pace think then? Why did he care? Fog clouded the window, and with it the weight of his past began to hang heavily on his shoulders. Unnecessary guilt gnawed at him as images of Mr. Rothberg's death consumed his thoughts. Now Dr. Dennis's sudden death. A man he'd never formally met, and his only contact, had died in this quiet town.

And all of it, a constant reminder life was fragile.

Tomorrow would be his first real, full day at Sam Heard Clinic. As he fell into a deep slumber, his last thoughts were that no matter what obstacles stood in his way, he wasn't going to fail. Not this time.

Chapter Two

Susan Pace cried all the way home and didn't stop until she parked in front of her two-story house at the edge of town. She had never done that before. She wasn't a crier. She wiped her nose. This new doctor was going to see who she was. She was no rookie when it came to people dismissing women doctors. She'd put up with that her whole life. It didn't matter that she'd been top of her class in med school. She'd been championed as a leader in Alzheimer's disease treatment, and she wasn't about to let anyone reprove a woman doctor without a fight.

She leaned over the seat and grabbed so many tissues from the little packet sitting on the passenger seat that she finally pulled out the last one, and then had to resort to wiping her eyes on the sleeve of her coat. She groaned in the silence of her car—unable to face the possibility that if Mark Moore's machine took over, it would be the end of her research and her career at Sam Heard Clinic.

She scrunched the last used hankie into her purse and stomped out of the car shaking her head. To top that off, she'd just lied to her best friend, Beverly, telling the ward clerk she was feeling ill, in order to leave the clinic earlier than usual. She sighed, heavily. What a wuss. Frankly, she couldn't imagine this new doctor Moore and his fancy machine being even a small reason for all this emotion. No, it was everything else piling up on her at once.

She got out and slammed the door, rubbing her temples to erase the thought. At least she'd kept her own studies at home in a locked steel cabinet right outside the kitchen, with all the data at her finger tips. Susan never trusted anyone with her work. She stumbled up the stairs. When she entered the foyer, the only thing she wanted to see was that steel 'Fort Knox,' with all her hard work safely tucked into its drawers. The figures from all her studies from the last five years were carefully documented on all her patients, those still at the clinic and the ones who had died or left. A friendly, but worried voice called out as she came in the front door, "Hey, how was your day?"

"Fine, Pam," Susan grumbled as she hung her coat on the coat tree.

Her sister, Pamela, stood in the archway that separated the dining room from the kitchen, carefully drying a pot, an apron tied around her waist.

"It doesn't sound that way. It sounds ominous."

Susan walked to her sister and hugged her. "Oh, you have no idea."

"Well, tell me. You want something to eat?"

"What are you offering?" Susan already knew. The entire house smelled of tomato sauce and garlic.

Pam gave her a knowing look and turned, walking briskly into the kitchen, Susan in tow behind her. "Spaghetti. I figured you could use it."

Susan closed her eyes and drew a steadying breath. "Oh, thank you." She paused as her gaze landed on the frail figure of her mother, seated in a wheelchair at the end of the long, formal dining room table. A spoon lay forgotten in her cereal bowl.

Susan slid into the seat next to her and pressed a kiss to her thinning silver hair.

"Hi, Ma. How are you feeling today?" Her mother didn't answer. Not even a flicker of recognition. Susan's stomach tightened as she called to her sister. "Is she eating at all?"

"A little. I think she likes to wait for you." Pamela came out with a generous plate of spaghetti and set it in front of Susan with deliberate care, the garlic bread crisp and golden at the side.

Susan forced a smile, but it didn't reach her eyes. "She's barely spoken in two weeks." The words hung between them, heavier than the silence that followed. She didn't want to think it—didn't dare say it out loud—but the fear lingered. Did her Ma even know who she was anymore?

Pamela's expression sharpened.

"Hey, you're not getting out of it that easy," she said, her voice firm but gentle. "Spill."

Susan studied her sister's face—those delicate features that people swore mirrored her own. In the right lighting, they could pass for twins. Right now, Pamela's eyes held fire.

"Tell me. What's he like?"

"Who?"

"Who?" Pamela rolled her eyes. "The new doctor."

"He looks like a conceited ass, but I could be wrong. I don't want to be judgmental, but I'm scared." Susan shook her head. "And Pammie, I'm worried—I really am. And it's the first time I've truly felt scared there."

"Scared?"

"Yes, someone put up a notice outside the breakroom that the clinic's having serious financial trouble and they're going to have to cut back. It was probably Phillip, but he has no balls, so of course he didn't sign his name to the bottom of it." She took a large spoon of spaghetti and twirled it, then shoved it into her mouth. "So good."

Pamela watched her. "Then why did Herman hire Mark Moore? Who was he planning on dumping before he died?"

"Me, probably." Susan wiped her face and picked up the spoon next to her mother. She scooped up a little cereal and offered it to the elderly woman, who barely opened her mouth wide enough to take in the nourishment. Susan turned to her sister, eyes brimming. "Why did no one bother to tell me how dire it all was? Why would Herman keep something like that from me?"

Her sister made a dismissive gesture and sank heavily into the chair across from Susan, the tension settling between them like an unspoken secret.

"Pam, it looks like things are so bad, we could close."

"Oh, honey, that's awful. Well, I guess they'll probably cut out my part-time nursing job. Maybe Brad can keep his. Oh, never mind my husband, this is just terrible."

"You want to hear the worst?"

"There's more?" Pam pursed her lips and put her head in her hands.

"They made Philip King the new chief." Susan ripped off a piece of garlic bread.

Pamela dropped her hands as her mouth turned into a sneer. "No! Over you?"

"I don't know what I'm going to do." Susan buttered the bread, then put it back on her plate.

Her mother jerked slightly, and a flicker of confusion crossed over her face. The subtle movement caught Susan's eye. She reached over gently and dabbed her mother's chin with the napkin, earning a grateful glance that tugged at her heart. Carefully, Susan folded the napkin back into her lap, fighting the sudden sting of tears.

She ate some more spaghetti and closed her eyes, but tears still dripped on her cheeks. "Oh, this is delicious. Nobody makes it like you do, Sis. It really hits the spot."

Pamela smiled. "Stop sniveling. I can't stand it when I don't know what to do to make you feel better, Sis." She got up. "Well, I've got to get home to Zoe. I want to put her to bed tonight. It's my turn. Then you and I are going to talk about this some more."

"I feel like such a fool," Susan admitted, her voice cracking. "I was horrid to the new guy, but Pam I don't care. It's as if they're already pushing me out the door."

A strong hand suddenly grabbed Susan's arm, and she shot a look to find her mother staring at her. "Not with the money Dad poured into that clinic. You're secure," her mother said. She and Pam both stared at their ma, stunned into silence. Joy mingled with disbelief, stealing Susan's breath for a heartbeat. At last, she found her voice, gentle and hesitant.

"Ma?"

"Ma?" Pamela echoed. She stood and moved around the table.

Susan moved, too, joining Pam in putting her arms around their mother.

Her mom asked, "How long do I have before…"

Susan exchanged a furtive glance at Pamela. "Two

weeks ago it lasted about five minutes, Ma," she answered.

"Then let me make them count." Her softly lined face pulled into a smile. "Susan, you can't mourn that other fellow forever, sweetheart. He was just a bum. He would have made things so much worse for you if you'd actually snagged him. I remember. I was there. I may have had problems since then, but I remember how hurt you were when he went back to his wife. You have to get over him. Who is this new man?"

So that was it? Her mother heard them talking, but couldn't react? Or did she hear the tail-end of their conversation? Susan tucked the thought away in the back of her mind to think about later. This had never happened before.

"He's a new doctor at the Clinic, Ma. They recruited him to start treating Alzheimer's in a different way. I'm worried the new head of the service will make me share my studies and my work with him so that the board will have to choose between him and me for the grant money. I don't think I can compete with something like this. He's new, his memory machine is new—and interesting. I just don't think I can do it, Ma."

Her mother huffed. "I can't believe I'm hearing this. All through medical school you competed. You were always top notch."

Her mother leaned toward her.

"Susan, I've told you a million times, you have to get along with colleagues." Her red-lined eyes searched Susan and her sister's faces. "I love you both so much. You know that don't you?"

"You know we do, Ma. And we love you," Pamela said.

Her mother stared at the empty cereal bowl. "You need to find out…" But her words cut off and in a moment she was silent again, back in that deep gorge where no one could reach her.

Pamela caught her breath. "I get so frightened when she does that. But I'm also grateful that she can come out of it, even for a little while. Susie, if she can come awake for a few minutes, then maybe she can come awake longer."

Susan leaned over the table and took her sister's hand. She shook her head, afraid to say what she was thinking for fear her mother just might understand. Instead, she whispered, "We both know that, unless…"

"Unless this Mark…and his machine." But Pamela stopped short as Susan gave her a warning look.

"Pammie, I-I know you're right, but I just can't deal with him right now." Susan pushed her empty plate back. "I ought to let this Mark Moore show me his machine and if it shows any success with our patients, I'd let Ma get on it and see if she's able to respond longer, remember better. That would be a true miracle."

"Well, you know you don't want to rattle what little security the place still has," Pamela said. "You need to see if it's even possible to work with him."

She patted Susan's hand. "Tomorrow I work twelve to six. Maybe I'll meet your new doc then and I can tell you what I think."

"That's what I'm afraid of," Susan said. "Tomorrow will tell—something. But right now, I'm going to bed."

Chapter Three

Mark was jolted awake by the blast of a horn. He grabbed his wrist watch off the coffee table and checked it. Six thirty a.m. He blinked and for a moment tried to remember where he was. Ironically, it was similar to the way his patients must feel when their minds failed them, and if they were relocated to a clinic, it could be especially dissociating. A new place, a new environment, would be intimidating to anyone.

The honking was relentless. Mark scrambled off the couch and shuffled to the door. When he opened it, a blast of winter wind pushed him back. He lowered his hand and saw a white sports car parked in front of the cabin, gleaming in the snow, and squinting through the windshield was a man in his early forties, with prematurely graying temples and sharp, blue eyes. Mark put up one finger, walked back into the cabin and pulled on his heavy overcoat. He found his boots under the coffee table and yanked them on.

When he opened the door again, the man was leaning against his car, arms folded, wrapped in a white wool topcoat, his hands snug in heavy black gloves, his feet encased in thick snow boots. He looked like a financier from New York who'd come to snow country to close a deal, but somehow, Mark doubted that was who he was.

The man rubbed his gloves together. "Cold! But at

least we've got a white Christmas, just like the song says." He stepped forward, extending a gloved hand. "Dr. Phillip King, new chief of Alzheimer's research. Dr. Moore, I presume?" Mark took his hand and nodded in affirmation.

"This is quite a ride." Mark nodded at the expensive sport car.

Dr. King wiped a spot off the hood. He gave Mark a practiced but polite smile and slapped him lightly on the shoulder as he edged him toward the passenger side. "Yes, well, welcome. Dr. Dennis gushed about you, and I wanted to introduce myself properly."

"Good to meet you, Dr. King."

"Likewise. I hope the cabin's been comfortable enough. I know it's not quite San Francisco, but it has its charm."

Mark glanced around at the barren trees, the leafless shrubbery. Unsure if "charm" was the right word, but he nodded. "It's peaceful. Exactly what I need for now."

"Good," Dr. King said, as he opened the passenger door. "Hop in. I wanted to stop by and personally welcome you to the team. Why don't I drive you to the clinic, and we can get to know each other a little better along the way?"

Mark checked his wrinkled clothes and Dr. King smirked.

"Slept in them. I was too exhausted to change," Mark explained. "But I'm good to go."

"You're fine. I want to introduce you to—a colleague, and five crusty old people who practically started this town. I'm thinking we can all sit down and talk about how we'll be working together."

Someone? Mark's guard shot up, but as he slid into

the seat, he had to admit—*curiosity was definitely getting the better of him.*

The conversation was professional, but before Mark could ask any more questions, he caught sight in a clearing of the same structure with debris around its frame that he'd passed on the way up to the clinic.

"What is that, or should I say, what was that, burned building?" He asked Dr. King.

"It's an eyesore all right," Dr. King answered, but didn't look in the direction Mark was pointing. "We think some crazy kids burned it down two years ago. Never got caught, but no one has the money or time to clean it up, I guess." He let out a shaky laugh, his tension unmistakable.

By the time they reached the clinic, the conversation had conveniently turned to topics centered around logistics—housing, clinic hours, and equipment. Mark couldn't shake the feeling that Dr. King was holding something back.

He glided the car into a spot next to the entrance. As Mark joined him on the stairs, Dr. King turned. "Dr. Moore, we've got heavier concerns than that scorched building."

Strange the doctor had turned the subject to the burned building. So it was a barn. Mark mentally shrugged. It didn't matter what the building was, but Dr. King finally was answering his question after avoiding it earlier. As he walked through the entrance, Mark's attention shifted to Susan Pace who stood at the reception desk, with Beverly behind it. The two women obviously waiting for them. His stomach tightened. Beverly nodded to Mark.

"Doctor, I need to get you your ID badge and room

key," she said. She disappeared through the side door.

Dr. King stepped forward with a grand gesture and patted Susan on the back. "Susan Pace, meet Dr. Mark Moore."

"We've met, Philip," Susan informed him, her gaze steady on Mark.

"Yes. An emergency," Mark added. "But I'm very familiar with Dr. Pace's work and approach to therapy." He spoke directly to Susan. "And I never got a chance to tell you yesterday, I've seen the accolades for your work with dementia patients." His stomach twisted into a knot of dread at the thought that this woman—this maddeningly, beautiful complication—could stand between him and the one breakthrough that had consumed his every waking hour.

Dr. King cleared his throat. "I didn't realize you two had already met, but in any case, I'd like to see both of you in my office right now. Members of the board want to meet you, Dr. Moore. We have big hopes for this clinic, and I believe the collaboration between your two approaches could be groundbreaking."

Mark exchanged a quick glance with Susan, and for the first time, he saw a flicker in her eyes—competition. This wasn't going to be easy. She didn't look like she played games. Well, neither did he.

"Shall we?" Dr. King gestured down the hallway.

Beverly dashed back through the side door and leaned over the counter. "Dr. Moore, whoa. Before you rush off, here's your ID card and your office key." Mark strutted back, and she handed them to him. She winked as he said, "Thanks," and grinned at her.

He clipped the ID to his shirt, all the while avoiding eye contact with Susan Pace. The memory of Angela humiliating him still fresh. But he wasn't going to let either of them have the satisfaction of seeing him worried or concerned. After pinning the ID to his shirt, he looked up brightly and said, "Lead the way." Then stopped abruptly.

"Something wrong?" Dr. King inquired.

"I'd like to check out my office, first," Mark said. Dr. King didn't answer but nodded.

"And I have a few things to clean up," Susan announced. Dr. King frowned, but nodded again as he silently walked down the hallway alone.

Susan turned to Mark after a quick look at Beverly. "Well, I'll see you in a few minutes, I guess." She marched down the hall with purpose, never looking back at Mark. He shot a glance at Beverly hoping for some explanation, but she shrugged, confusion etched across her face.

****

A quick knock on her door roused Susan. Bev stood in the frame, two Styrofoam cups in her hands. "How about some coffee before you tackle the meeting this morning?" she asked, stepping into the office.

Susan stood and extended both arms out to her friend. She took the coffee. "Not looking forward to that. And on top of it all, I've only got two patients left, Bev." She slurped from the cup. "This just does it."

Beverly smiled. "Mark seems enthusiastic. Aren't you two the busy little bees?"

Susan met her gaze but said nothing, her lips pressed into a thin line."

"Okay, what's going on?" Beverly took a seat.

Susan held the cup with both hands and rested it on her stomach as she sat. "What do you mean? Nothing.

There's nothing to tell, Bev. He's a narcissistic, egotistical…I don't know what."

"Well, there's an awful lot of emotion going on between you for him to just be a narcissistic, egotistical whatever. When's the wedding?"

"Stop." Susan took another sip and put the cup on the blotter. "I'm focusing on my job right now, and he's the one that could rip it out from under me."

"Is that a fact? Well it feels like electricity every time I see you two together. And he just got here." She sipped her coffee, looking over the rim at Susan.

"Yeah, well, I promise you'll be the first to know," Susan smirked. "I got work to do. I'll see you for lunch."

Beverly got up. "Got the message." She looked mockingly disappointed, winked at Susan and left, closing the door behind her.

After another large gulp of coffee, Susan took out a legal pad and a pen, her go-to rescue from feeling overwhelmed. Her mind replaying the repartee with Mr. Johnson. The unspoken rivalry between her and Mark must be so obvious. Nurse Emily had appeared uncomfortable when she watched them quibbling yesterday. She even blushed. Rodney seemed to have trouble mumbling a 'good morning' without turning red, and finally her best friend, Bev, chomped at the bit hoping for juicy gossip—even though there wasn't any—not yet. *Where did that come from.* She was not attracted to the man.

She rubbed her face, but before she had a chance to work out the next phase of this 'unworkable' plan, a sharp rap broke her focus. Bev again? Susan tossed the pen down. She loved Bev, but this was getting a little much.

"Come in," she ordered, slightly exasperated. The door opened slowly, and Mark's head peeked out from behind it.

"Dr. Moore," she said, realizing she sounded awkward. "What do you…need?"

Mark opened the door and leaned against it holding two Styrofoam cups of coffee in his hands. Susan stood.

"Wasn't sure whether or not you took two sugars and cream, just cream, or black."

She smiled in a way she hadn't wanted to. "Are you saying I need some sugar?" *Stop flirting. I don't care for him. His shoulders are almost bigger than his ego.* She pressed her lips into a thin line so he wouldn't see her drooling.

"Ah, another bone of contention."

Susan picked up the cup Beverly had just brought her and shook it in front of him. "Someone beat you to the punch," she took a loud sip.

"Can't win 'em all." He stood there holding the cups, looking awkwardly adorable. *Stop it. Get ahold of yourself. You will not fall for another doctor, no matter how handsome he is.*

"Is there something else?" She stared at him over the rim of the cup.

Mark stepped inside and set the extra cup on the corner of her desk. From his coat pocket, he pulled out a key and gave it a little jiggle, eyebrows raised. "My office. Could you please show me where it is?"

Susan stepped out from behind her desk, unable to hold back a slight, ever so delicate, grin. She pointed to the cup of coffee he'd put on her desk. "Oh, so this was a bribe?"

"I'll never tell."

"Uh-huh. Okay, I'll be happy to take you. I'm sure you'll want to get settled in before we dive into *our* work." She gently put the coffee cup in a wastebasket next to her desk.

He saluted with the remaining cup. "Gotcha. After you."

****

Mark couldn't help glancing at her well-toned body as he followed her down the hallway slowly, silently. He had to admit he was enjoying the way the curves of her back and legs swayed from side-to-side as if she were baiting him. Her pace was brisk, her black ponytail bouncing slightly with each step. He was intrigued that she did not look back to check whether or not he was following. Or was it she wouldn't give him the satisfaction? He smirked. How could anyone not admire her perfect posture? Like a dancer.

Yesterday, she'd shown him a sharp demeanor, confidence, and all of it very attractive, but there was something different about her today, though she had opened up a bit, that went well beyond her discomfort with him.

Suddenly, Susan stopped so abruptly he almost bumped into her. "Here we are," she said a little too blithely.

They'd reached the end of the hallway, and he noticed the office was a corner one. Without looking at him, Susan put a hand out for the key. He placed it in her palm, and she inserted it into the lock and opened the door. Robotically, she stood aside to let him enter. It felt, somehow, as though she saw right through him—as if all the titles and trappings he'd been handed belonged to someone else. Someone wiser. Someone worthy.

In any case, he turned his attention to his new office. It was spacious, far larger than he'd expected. Natural light poured in from a large window and bathed the room in a golden hue. He walked across the room and saw the window overlooked another breathtaking view—the lake that stretched out endlessly.

"Wow," Mark murmured. He turned and brushed his hand over a gorgeous mahogany wood desk with highly polished Spanish style curlicue legs, that took center stage in front of the window. A Tiffany lamp sat in a corner. His gaze scanned the rest of the room. Built in bookshelves lined the walls, filled with mostly medical journals and anthologies. A stand-alone bar sat in the corner, all clean lines and quiet arrogance. The whiskey was expensive—too expensive for a clinic.

"Too fancy for me," Mark noted as he turned to Susan.

She clutched the back of a visitor chair, her face pale. "I just wasn't expecting this, is all," he tried to explain, pretending not to notice her uneasiness. He thumbed back at the bar. "If that bar is operational, we might need a shot of all that good stuff while we work together—I, for one, could use a little help right now."

She forced a smile and stood a little straighter, as if she were composing herself. She wasn't fooling Mark. He instinctively knew what was happening.

"Yeah, no kidding," she said, her voice cracking. "It's just that this office is special." She picked up a framed picture sitting on the edge of the desk and held it to her chest before Mark could see what it was.

"Let me guess. This was Dr. Dennis's office?"

Bright tears appeared in her eyes. "Yes. It was."

Mark put his coffee cup down on the blotter and

moved over to her. He took her by both shoulders. "Look, honestly, I'll be happy to trade offices with you, if it would make you feel better."

"That's very kind of you, but no, no, it's not necessary." She pulled her mouth into a smile. "Dr. Dennis loved to joke and say outrageous things—like, if anything ever happened to him, this office should be assigned to the person who looked like they'd make the biggest impact on Sam Heard Clinic. I think he was expecting someone here to win a Nobel Prize for medicine or something." She chuckled then caught herself and stood stick straight again. Even though she obviously tried to sound unimpressed, there was a slight edge in her voice. "And apparently, that's you."

Mark caught a faint hint of something else in her tone, too. Jealousy, perhaps?

"I didn't realize I'd be getting the royal treatment."

"Well, I'm sure with your…machine, you'll need the extra space for your figures, right?" But it seemed to him that she recovered her composure too quickly, and when she reached the door, she turned and pointed to his desk. "I think your coffee cup made a stain on your new blotter."

Mark picked up the cup.

"You may be—"

She didn't wait for an answer, but stepped into the hallway, then apparently changing her mind, turned back into the office. Mark stared at her quizzically.

"Back so soon?" he quipped.

"I'm sure this meeting is about Dr. King wanting us to collaborate," Susan said tentatively, "but I won't have my work undermined."

Mark met her gaze, "Let me assure you, both our

therapies will be respected, Susan."

Just as she was about to close the door again, Dr. King pushed it open, a quizzical look on his face. "Excuse me," the new Chief said sharply, stepping in front of Susan. "I believe I mentioned I wanted the two of you in my office." He checked his watch with theatrical precision, disapproval radiated off him in waves. "Half an hour ago."

Mark didn't argue. He stepped with them into the hallway, his strides measured but tense. In front of him, Dr. King's footsteps echoed—slower, heavier, like marching toward the gallows.

With every step, the weight on Mark's shoulders grew heavier. It was becoming clear: the path forward wasn't just uphill. It was a battlefield.

He suspected the real problem. Money. The enzyme he used with the machine was expensive and hard to recreate.

Dr. King fell into step with Mark, but noticing Susan wasn't with them, Mark glanced over his shoulder. She shot him a warning look, as if she knew how tenuous the new Chief's temperament could be. When they reached Dr. King's office, he stumbled inside, leaving door open.

Mark paused for a moment, his attention drawn to a glass display case mounted on the wall just outside the office. Snapshots of birthday parties, office parties, Christmas parties, with some of the people he had just met, including Beverly and Emily. Susan's picture was there, taken when she was only slightly younger, and dressed in a Halloween costume, wearing a black witch's hat, with her tongue stuck out, her arm around a tall, lean older man with graying temples and a roguish smile. Underneath the caption was written, *Dr. Pace and Dr.*

Dennis frightening the staff.

In yet another picture taken at a former Christmas party, people raised glasses in cheer, and Dr. Dennis, donning whiskers and a Santa Claus Suit, was handing out presents to the little children from the town who were sitting on his lap. The last photo appeared to be Susan with Dr. Dennis clearly together at his fortieth birthday party, the doctor blowing out candles, their arms entwined around each other, broad grins on their faces, sitting at a white-linen-draped table with white carnations in a crystal vase in the center.

Mark leaned in closer to look at the photo. There was no question who it was. Bright, overhead lights illuminated Susan's gorgeous silky hair. And she and Dr. Dennis seemed...close. Not just the typical professional rapport he'd seen between other colleagues, but something more. Perhaps a lot more. For a brief moment, Mark flashed on a thought that he might know the root of her hostility.

Susan's voice from behind startled him. "That was taken two years ago."

He turned. Her expression was unreadable.

"I'm sorry," he said." I didn't mean to embarrass you. So, you and Dr. Dennis worked together quite a bit."

"Quite a bit." Susan's lips quivered.

Dr. King sidled up to them, that same phony grin crossing his lips, but clearly anger surfacing. "Dr. Dennis was certainly a mentor to her. He was a great man."

Susan interjected, sounding somewhat annoyed. "We worked together for a couple of years before he"— she shook her head—"yesterday."

Dr. King strutted back into his office. "Well, come on in." He took his place behind his desk and sank into the oversized desk chair—more like a throne than a seat—its high back and overstuffed arms swallowing him whole. Mark followed, but Susan stayed in the hallway.

When Mark sneaked a peek, Susan's cheeks burned red, and her glare could have melted steel. He couldn't decide if he was more worried or impressed. But she finally sauntered past him into the room and stood behind a visitor chair. Both of them faced the new Chief.

"Yep," Dr. King said, looking down at his desk. "It's a shocker all right. I plan on attending the funeral, of course. But on a lighter note, Dr. Moore—" He stopped and took a breath, broadening his smile. "—Or rather, Mark—" emphasizing his name. "—Let me just say that we celebrate everything around here. If your work is as distinguished as I expect, we'll be celebrating your groundbreaking memory machine"—he chuckled—"if it works."

If it works. The magic words Mark tried to avoid. *Talk about pressure?* "Yes, sir," Mark said.

As Mark took in the office, he recalled his Aunt Jenny's descent into Alzheimer's. That was the trigger that had fueled his research. Memories of Angela flooded his brain also. How she encouraged him, ostensibly believing in him, only to discover she was stealing his research.

"We all know about the debacle in San Francisco," Dr. King announced as he sat with his fingers entwined across his stomach. "So you don't have to excuse yourself to any of us. We know the ins and outs of bureaucracy."

Mark didn't miss the sly smirk he gave Susan.

"You either prove yourself immediately, or you're

out. That's the unspoken expectation, isn't it?" Dr. King stared into Mark's eyes. "Let me rephrase that. You prove yourself, and we'll help you in any way we can. No one here is out to get you."

It was getting worse and worse, but Mark decided to take the optimistic point of view rather than what the doctor was really saying to him. Thoughts of Dr. Dennis and his idyllic dream of offering hope in the fight against Alzheimer's—stood in sharp contrast to the quiet threat from Dr. King: if he failed, he'd be out on his ear.

"Come on up here, I'm expecting great things," were the last words Dr. Dennis had said to Mark on the phone. If only Dr. King had heard those words.

****

Susan found herself fuming, unable to settle into the so-called meeting. It hadn't gotten past her that as they'd headed toward Dr. King's office just now, Mark and Phillip had moved down the hall, leaving her behind. To make matters worse, Dr. King, a man who had been clearly subordinate to her at the clinic and who knew very little about Alzheimer's, had the nerve to advise her of this so-called meeting by phone only a few hours ago. It was not a request; he was throwing his new-found weight around. She could feel her lips tensing unable to conceal her anger. Was King planning on replacing her with Mark Moore?

"Well, come on in, get comfortable," Mark had called to her, pulling out the second visitor chair.

That did it. She couldn't stand the disingenuousness, but she strutted in and plopped into the chair without looking at him. Dr. Dennis had promised her a fair shake to show off her talk therapy. What had happened to that? He'd even assured her she would get a unique chance to write up her own study for the prestigious medical journal he'd been a part of. *Her own study, not one shared with this new doctor.* And what about clinic head? Who'd hired King? Dr. Dennis had died so quickly she wasn't even sure how Phillip got the job. She wasn't a petty person, but she was miffed that no one had even offered her a chance to be the head if Dr. Dennis were no longer there. And now here was this green-eyed, six-foot one, interloper with scruffy, blond hair, *not that she'd noticed,* who was about to take away her thunder.

Susan couldn't concentrate on Dr. King's words. In fact, she never heard them at all. Her attention was on her nemesis, and he met her gaze with a cool stare. Why would she even notice him scanning her like a hot lunch, as if she were one of the countless girls undoubtedly swooning over him. Well, not her, not now, not ever. She had a job to protect.

Dr. King shifted behind his desk. Susan guessed he was trying to project authority, but it felt forced—a demand for respect, earned or not. And as he droned on all she could think about was Mark storming into the clinic with his precious memory machine.

"Well, first and foremost, I sincerely want to thank the two of you for coming into this meeting."

Oh, sure, as if we had a choice.

"And I want to thank you both for committing yourselves to this work." Susan heard Phillip's business-like tone to make himself more important than he was. His thin lips coaxed into a phony smile. "I won't waste time. We need to secure government funding for this clinic, and we need it fast. We're depending on the two of you."

"What?" Susan stared at him, the air crackling with

tension.

"That's what I was hoping my machine would accomplish," Mark interrupted, his voice hard as steel. "I assumed Dr. Dennis brought me here to elevate the clinic's profile—to broaden its influence in dementia treatment. That's what I thought, anyway—to make the clinic renowned for cutting-edge studies. So, I really don't need anyone meddling in my work—"

Susan almost jumped out of the chair. "Oh, brother, are you kind to yourself. What is this machine? The holy grail of dementia research, utterly disregarding all the years of work I put into perfecting talk therapy methods?" Susan leaned across Dr. King's desk. This meeting was only going to make matters worse. She glanced back at Mark who looked so self-satisfied she could smack him.

"Meddling? You think you can waltz in here with your fancy machine and just erase years of patient care?" She snapped. "My therapy works because it treats the human side of dementia, not just the disease."

"Enough." Dr. King rose partway from his chair, his voice slicing through the air like a scalpel. Susan straightened instinctively, her spine stiffening beneath his glare.

He looked between them—first Susan, then Mark—disappointment etched in every controlled breath.

"I warned Dr. Dennis this might happen," he said coldly. "And this is exactly why you're both sitting here now. The government isn't going to bankroll a one-dimensional approach."

Then, turning his attention to Mark, he added with a clipped nod. "She's not entirely wrong."

Mark leaned forward, tension pulling across his

brow as a frown settled in. The words stung more than he wanted to admit.

"Look a machine isn't going to be enough to show we are making progress with the disease. I'm sorry, Mark. They want results multidimensionally. And they want collaboration."

Mark let out a long breath, then raised his eyes to meet Dr. King's. "May I at least explain exactly what will happen when the enzyme is reintroduced to the part of the brain that fuels Alzheimer's?"

Susan lowered her eyes. She'd said what she'd wanted to say ever since she heard he was coming to Crescent Hill.

"My machine can be thought of as a brain booster. It will double IQ, skyrocket energy levels, and connect areas of the brain that were previously diminished."

"Okay," Susan blurted out. "But is it safe?"

"While I was in San Francisco, I led a team of neuroscience experts working tirelessly to reintroduce an enzyme that gets lost as we age. The trials on mice worked exceptionally. But the first human patient died of an undiagnosed heart ailment, not from the machine. He died three days after working with him, and during that time his memory continued to improve."

"So Dr. Dennis invited you to come up here with your—your machine, which may or may not have killed someone—in order to try it out on our patients?" Her eyes flared and she folded her arms over her chest.

Mark stood. "I explained to him exactly what I just told you. He felt the machine had not gotten a fair shake, and he wanted to see for himself what it could do for Alzheimer's patients."

For a moment, Susan reflected on all she'd just

heard. By making her work with Mark and with two separate therapies going at the same time—it reeked of desperation. When did the clinic's future become so precarious?

"Okay, I think we can clear up some of this animosity right now," Dr. King said.

Susan gazed at him in disbelief. While Mark looked at Dr. King—innocently, like a puppy who'd been reprimanded for soiling the carpet. Now what was Phillip up to? Surely, he wasn't going to bring *that* up, was he?"

"Clear up what?" Mark asked

Dr. King tented his hands, lowered his head, and stared directly at Susan.

She could feel her stomach roiling. He wouldn't. He couldn't.

"Susan, may I explain your situation?"

She gave Phillip a glare that could peel paint. "You're not really going to do this?"

Philip stared at her expectantly.

"Okay, then I can explain my own situation, thank you very much."

Dr. King held out a palm and offered her center stage. Susan turned partially to address Mark. "My mother, Eleanor"—she hesitated to stem her tears, but forced herself to continue—"is in the second stages of Alzheimer's."

"I'm very sorry to hear this."

"I didn't mention to anyone that it's possible my mother's dementia could be because my dad disappeared, and I think she's blocking out why." Susan continued, "Her memory loss has gotten more acute recently, and I'm afraid something important might have come up to prompt that." She hesitated, searching her own memory.

****

Mark waited a moment before he answered. Susan looked ethereal, someone he wanted to help, but he couldn't figure out how. "I'm not sure what you're suggesting. Do you think the machine might assist her in bringing lost memories to light?"

"No, I'm afraid it won't, but—" Her eyes glistened. "—Maybe it could. I would do anything to stem this memory loss, but I refuse to let her get hurt, mentally and physically."

Mark stood and held on to the back of his chair. His mind racing. Now she didn't appear so much a rival or a fellow doctor, but as a woman—a daughter, fighting desperately for her mother's survival. Perhaps she'd suspected this compassionate side of him, especially after seeing it with that first patient, Mr. Johnson.

She wasn't saying anything—but she didn't have to. Mark felt the full weight of her confession settle between them like a storm cloud, heavy with everything she hadn't said aloud. Now that he knew, the pieces clicked into place. This wasn't just about him coming with a new therapy, trying to replace her. Oh, no, this was personal. Intimate. A wound she carried.

His chest tightened as he looked at her. He wanted to hold her, tell her everything would be all right—which was stupid, he couldn't do that. Sympathy stirred in him, sure—but something else tangled with it. A low, unspoken tension between them. He tried to tamp it down, that mix of anger, regret…and desire. He could see it in the flicker of her gaze, in the way she looked at him like she wanted to run—or reach for him. And God help him, he felt it, too. Every muscle in his body was coiled, caught between stepping back—and pulling her in.

Mark scratched his head, biding for time. "Look, I think the most important person to demonstrate the machine is Mr. Johnson right now. Let's see if he can tolerate it. I mean, he's the one in obvious distress. Then, if you like what you see, we can put your mother on it."

Mark noticed the flicker of disapproval in Dr. King's eyes—a subtle tightening of his jaw, the kind of frown that came from being challenged without ever being directly opposed. Mark hadn't meant to overstep. He wasn't here to disrupt the hierarchy. He just wanted the machine to speak for itself. To rise above the noise. To prove, without a shadow of doubt, that it worked. He smiled and tried to ground himself.

Maybe Dr. King had misread the heat in his voice—because the new boss's response came quick and clinical. "I hear you," he said, "but honestly, I think right now we should use someone less...volatile."

"May I suggest Gertie Fuller," Susan countered. "Her husband, Harold, died. Gertie gets extremely agitated when I ask her about him."

"Yet another bone of contention?" Mark noted. Truthfully, he thought there would be plenty more. The corners of Susan's mouth turned up into a small grin, for the first time, and it was glorious.

"Okay," Dr. King interrupted, obviously encouraged by her softening. "It's up to you two now," he said, standing and then just as suddenly, sitting again. "Just make up your minds."

"Easier said than done, sir," Mark said. An uncomfortable silence followed. "Okay, look," Mark offered. "Truce. Gertie Fuller will be the first subject on the machine, if I am allowed to work with the machine alone this first time out? Deal?"

Susan hesitated, her expression tightening. For a moment, Mark thought she might refuse—that he'd crossed a line he couldn't uncross. But then she stood, brushing her hands down her sides as if shaking off the weight of her uncertainty.

"You drive a hard bargain," she said, her face stoic again. "But okay. Just this once."

She extended a hand without making eye contact. It was quick, firm, and decisive. Then she looked into his face, and the spark in her eyes caught him off guard. Fierce. Compassionate. Beautiful.

"And they aren't *subjects*, Dr. Moore," she added, voice low but pointed. "They're patients."

Mark took her hand, her words echoing in his head. Patients. Not data points. It shouldn't have mattered—but somehow, coming from her, it did.

"I meant 'patients.' And would you *please* call me Mark." He let out an audible sigh.

"Fine, Mark." Her voice held a note of surrender—not defeat, just a gentle easing. Whatever lay ahead, it wouldn't be a war. Not now. He caught the change and gave a slight nod, as if tipping his hat to the small victory.

Dr. King planted both hands flat on the desk, the sharp sound punctuating the silence. Then he pushed to his feet with the kind of finality that left no room for debate.

Mark turned to her. "Remember, we agreed just now, Gertie Fuller will be on the machine exclusively. I won't have my work diluted by—"

"Diluted?" Susan's voice rose even sharper.

Mark jumped back, holding his hands up, palms out

"Sorry. I didn't mean it that way—"

Susan interrupted. "You act like I'm some amateur, Mark. These patients need more than your clinical detachment," she said, her voice barely controlled. "I've worked too hard to be sidelined by a machine."

"And I didn't come here to coddle patients while they reminisce about their pasts." Mark's glare was icy. "I came here to enhance their treatment."

Susan's dark eyes narrowed. "Enhance, or replace?"

Dr. King pounded his hands on his desk. He glared at them. "Look, I don't care what you think of each other or your methods. The fact is, we're on the verge of losing our funding. If we don't secure that government grant, this clinic is done, and so are your precious careers."

Mark's expression turned cold and tense silence filled the room. He hoped Susan didn't see the flicker of fear. She'd probably chalk it up to his bruised ego, but he knew different.

Dr. King folded his arms and leaned forward, his expression darkening. "You will work together," he continued. "I don't care how. Combine your methods. Strengthen your results. Prove that this clinic has something unique to offer—a blend of cutting-edge technology and compassionate, patient-centered care." He leaned across his desk, eyes on fire. "My reputation is on the line, too. So, you two will do what's necessary, or I'll find others who will."

Mark had had enough. He could feel his expression, stubborn, childish, but he couldn't help himself. "I'm not compromising the integrity of my work."

"Well, neither am I, Doctor," Susan shot back. "This will only work if we both have equal say."

Dr. King brushed by them and stomped out to the

hallway, then turned. "I want positive actions. And make no mistake, Doctors, I expect results—and quickly. That's all I have to say."

Mark figured Dr. King's patience had worn thin. Until they had concrete results—proof that the memory machine and her therapy worked together, until he could see progress, the two of them were nothing more than a distraction.

Chapter Four

Oh, it wasn't even close to being settled for Susan. She stormed out of the office before Mark, his gaze burning into her back, and when they reached the reception desk and he touched her shoulder lightly, she spun around to face him, pushing his hand off her like an unwanted bug, her eyes blazing.

"Don't touch me." The words came out sharper than she meant, but Mark had crossed a line—and he needed to know it. *No, he makes me feel…something for him.*

"Excuse me." It sounded obsequious.

She could see his ire. She'd made him mad. Good, but it looked like he wasn't through.

"You're treating this like it's a psychological experiment, Susan," he shot back, his voice low, intense."

She felt the blood rush to her face. The audacity. The arrogance. The nerve. She spun away from him before she said something she'd regret. Even now, she wanted to smooth the lock of hair that had fallen on his forehead. She fisted her hands to keep from touching him.

Behind the counter, Beverly looked like she'd rather disappear than watch the tension unfold. She was stiff, uneasy, as if she were trapped courtside at a match that was turning brutally personal.

Susan drew a breath, deep and steady—but her voice, when she spoke, still carried the burden of too many emotions at once.

"It's not about psychotherapy," she said tightly. "It's about *dignity*."

"I think you two should settle this somewhere else," Beverly offered. "I don't mean to interfere, but patients can overhear your squabbling."

"I agree," Susan said, backing into the glass double doors with just enough force that they swung wide open.

Mark glanced at Beverly. "Okay, then I guess we'll be taking it outside," he said.

The door almost hit Mark in the face as he grabbed it and stepped out onto wet terrazzo.

Brushing snow off the bench with a sweep of her hand, Susan sat down hard, arms crossed, and lower lip just shy of a pout.

Mark sat next to her, leaving a slight space between them.

The moment he sat down, Susan hunched over. Her body language made her seem softer, or her fury had exhausted itself, he couldn't tell which. They sat in silence for a long moment, the kind of silence that only came with years of knowing each other, and yet they'd only been introduced a day ago.

"My mother's dying." Susan sat back, her eyes searching the misty sky. "You think I'm unaware of all the work you've put into this? I know how hard it all is, but what about the patients who won't benefit from your machine? The ones who are too far gone? Sometimes, maybe just hearing the human voice is the only thing that keeps them tethered to who they were, until, until…the end."

"Let's not go there," Mark said. He spread his arms across the back of the bench. It felt like she was shifting.

Looking at her profile, her features so even, so delicate, he couldn't stop circling back to the way she'd said his name—*Mark*. It lodged in his chest like a promise and seemed like a soft, deliberate move toward something that might—finally—become a collaboration.

He needed her to get it—really get it—in a way no one in the Bay Area ever had. The politics, the pressure, the fine line he walked every damn day. Because Angela had not gotten it, not at all. When he turned to face Susan, and looked into her eyes, steady and clear, he saw something he hadn't dared hope for: maybe understanding. Not pity. Not skepticism. Just…her. Seeing him. It made him hopeful.

"I hope you aren't planning on using our patients as guinea pigs to further your career."

His jaw tightened. Oh, hell. She wasn't ready to get it after all. "That's not fair, any more than you using old people to demonstrate your compassion."

"You think I wouldn't give everything I have to fix this? To fix Mother? But there's no miracle cure, Mark. There's just hope…and people like you, looking for something to hang your reputation on."

"I'm not your enemy." He sat forward and shot back. "I'm sure there were people here who resented your work, your ability."

She paused. He waited expecting another pushback of him and his machine. Her words broke into his thoughts.

"I loved Herman Dennis." There, her admission was—unguarded, unexpected. Hanging in the air like a confession she hadn't prepared for. Susan stared into his eyes. "Dr. Dennis and I…were engaged."

The words hit him like a gut punch. "I think it was

pretty obvious you two might have been together, but…engaged?" He felt a flood of emotions—anger, jealousy, confusion.

She obviously didn't notice his concern, or didn't want to address it, clearly locked up in her own story as she continued, "It all started when I first came to the clinic. He never wore a ring. He had an apartment in town. He let me believe he was divorced. I had no idea he was still with his wife for the sake of their kids."

Mark's mind raced. Dr. Dennis—the man who had believed in his work, had encouraged his research—was also the man who had lied to Susan? Talk about two worlds colliding.

"I kind of wish I'd known all this. It would have made our introduction a lot easier." He looked down abashed.

"It's not really any of your business and frankly, when he told me he was hiring you, I thought he wanted to strengthen the ward, with new blood, and I might get a fresh start. I wanted one. Just like you. And also, well, after what just happened to him—I still can't say he died, I didn't want his memory to be marred. He was a wonderful man,"

Mark wasn't sure what he wanted to do; hold her, get out of there before he got himself into another flawed relationship? "What were you thinking?" he stammered. "That you'd punish yourself?"

Susan swallowed hard. Her voice broke. Mark pulled her to him and kissed her hard.

"Why did you do that?" Her face whitened. He wanted to tell her it was a kiss fueled by all the emotions he'd kept bottled up since meeting her.

They slowly broke away. "I'm sorry. But just so you

know, there's no judgement here."

Susan cast her eyes down. "I'm a professional. I don't flirt. Let's just go forward, and get this going and…and start with Gertie." She got up, leaving Mark sitting on the bench. He watched her yet again walk down the embankment, this time slowly, and in a few moments, the car's headlights cast long, golden streaks across the fading pavement.

****

Susan held the wheel loosely, but her chest was tight—too tight. "What? Why had she let him kiss her? How dare he? She needed to make him see she'd spent months using her talk and music therapy to try to reach her mother. But to no avail. The clinical tools she trusted most hadn't been enough.

She wasn't ready to admit that out loud—not yet— but in the quiet hum of the engine, something unspoken rose to the surface. She loved that he'd kissed her like that. It was a moment when emotion made her feel alive. His lips so moist and tender. She felt herself getting excited just thinking about it. Now their relationship would get even more complicated. Maybe she'd even have to concede the fact that possibly she wasn't the smartest person in the room anymore. Maybe there was another way…and dammit, maybe it was Mark's way.

She exhaled, slow and low.

This machine might be the only chance they'd have to save her mother, the clinic, and the other patients.

Everything she'd built…everything she was fighting for…might now depend on the one man she initially couldn't stand—and yet now couldn't stop thinking about.

She had to admit, she'd never seen such unyielding

determination as he had shown. He was aggressive. She could learn from that. He could learn humility from her, too. When she reached the house, she turned off the ignition and sat for a moment, staring out the windshield. The house looked surreal with that deep green wreath Pammie and Zoe had made just for her fastened to the door. It had been transformed into a perfect Christmas postcard scene.

She'd make this work. She'd find a way to combine their therapies.

If she didn't strangle him first.

****

Pamela opened the door carrying Zoe and a child's car seat. She waved at Susan as she came down the stairs to her car and buckled the child into the backseat. The little girl kicked her chubby legs into the air and gave a delighted squeal, seeing Susan.

"Tootie, Tootie," she called out. Susan stepped onto the frozen pavement and made a bee line over to press a big kiss on Zoe's head. "Hi, baby girl," she said, holding the child's face in her hands. She looked over at Pam, tired and heaving long breaths.

"Thanks," she said softly. "I owe you."

Pamela waved it off. "You owe me nothing. Besides, Brad's on the late shift again, and Zoe didn't nap. So I'm running on fumes. It would have been the same anyway we cut it."

Susan kissed her sister. She knew there was more going on between Pam and her husband—Susan could feel it—but now wasn't the time. Not with their mother, Eleanor, inside waiting for her and the weight of the day still sitting heavily on her chest.

"Get some rest," Susan murmured. "We'll talk

tomorrow."

Pamela nodded, hugged her sister again, quickly, and drove off into the dark.

Once inside, with the comfort of warmth wrapping around her like a shawl, Susan gently reheated a bowl of soup. She set it before her mother, the scent rising in soft, familiar waves.

They sat in silence. Her mother stared at the table, unmoving, while Susan lifted each spoonful with care, guiding it to lips that barely parted.

It wasn't the meal that mattered. It was the act. The love, the grief, the history between them—all carried in that quiet rhythm of feeding and waiting.

Susan made sure that every slurp of the soup was taken in and swallowed. Dementia sufferers could choke if the liquid went down wrong.

She tried to stay present. Tried to focus on feeding her mother, not on the chill outside the window, or on the way the shadows stretched long across the floor.

When her mother had finished eating, Susan cleared the table, but her mind kept drifting back to Mark. To the heat in his voice. The fire in his eyes. Passion pushed people forward, made them determined. And he had that. There was something she'd never considered before: grief can be abated by fantasy and maybe that's what she was doing now—seeing Mark's sexuality so that she didn't have to focus on what was right in front of her. She came back to the table and sat.

"Hey, you want to get in bed?" She didn't expect an answer and got none, but helped her mother walk down the hall to her bedroom. When Susan finished undressing her, helping her brush her teeth and wash her face, she tucked her mother into bed. Same routine each night, but

Susan would do anything for her mom. She was about to turn off the side table light when her mother threw off her covers and twisted atop the blankets, arms restless, eyes darting toward the window as if waiting for someone—or trying to escape someone only she could see.

"Ma, what's bothering you? Do you hurt somewhere?" Susan sat on the side of the bed, but her mother didn't answer. No matter how gently Susan tried to communicate with her, her mom remained unresponsive, trapped in silence. "Oh, Ma, I wish we could escape to Carmel again."

Her mother turned and grabbed Susan's arm. "I miss Walter," she suddenly blurted. Susan grabbed her mother and hugged her—tight.

"Oh, Ma, I know. Remember how much fun you, me, Pammie, and Daddy had before he left that summer? But, Ma, Dad's still around. We'll see him again, I'm sure of it." She smoothed her mother's hair and helped her scoot under the covers. Then she whispered a lullaby neither of them had sung in years. In a few moments, she heard her mother's soft snoozing. She pressed a kiss to her forehead, lingering there longer than she meant to. Then she switched the light off and lingered in the doorway, wondering not for the first time if she was in over her head.

The night clock glowed faintly, casting a soft halo across the worn photo frame next to it.

And there he was.

Walter Pace.

Tall. Handsome. Smiling through the photo with that same charm that used to turn heads—and then disappeared just as fast.

He'd vanished one summer without warning, leaving behind a wife and two teenagers and a trail of stories heard second-hand from shopkeepers that no one could quite verify. No phone call. Just absence.

Susan stared at his photo for a moment, heart tight with a familiar, useless ache. She didn't even know if he was alive. But sometimes—like now—she imagined he was out there. Watching. Regretting.

She turned away before the old anger could rise again and slipped quietly out of the room.

****

Mark sauntered back to his office, in no hurry to be alone after the tension between him and Susan. His work was too important, but that didn't stop his mind from wondering if her skin felt as soft as it looked. Or if she'd file a harassment suit against him because of that heady kiss.

Gah. He had to stop fantasizing about her, but once inside the safety of his private space, he leaned against the door. Memories of Angela tricking him poured in, colliding with Mark's hope that Susan wasn't like his ex.

Carolers in the distance reminded him of last Christmas. The singing and presents and lighted trees around San Francisco, Union Square, the department store on Market Street that had revolving Christmas stories played out by dolls in the windows. He and Angela got all bundled up and stood arm in arm, wrapped in warm coats, scarves and heavy wool gloves, knit hats on their heads. He thought he'd live his whole life with her. He just hadn't seen her betrayal coming or he'd ignored it because he'd been blinded by love.

Now with Christmas cheer outside his window here in Crescent Hill, maybe different feelings were emerging, like suspicion that something wasn't right. He'd been brought up here on a whim. No, no, no. He suddenly decided to think positively. It was thoughts of Angela that put him in these negative spaces, and it was going to stop. Besides, Aunt Jenny would have encouraged him to see the beauty of the season mixed with the excitement of his new work with Susan as a way to win all around. If that happened, it would be a true miracle. It would mean perhaps he could also win over the funding committee.

Chapter Five

A gray, colorless young man, with a round, greasy face burst in on Mark the next morning, unannounced and with a chart in his hands. "Greetings," he said, "I'm Susan's assistant, Eric Forrester. We haven't met, so, yeah, hi."

Mark hadn't time to put on his white jacket. He hated people bursting in on him without knocking, but once he saw the assistant, he understood why. He'd seen the man roaming the halls with Susan that first day, but no one had introduced him, and Mark had no idea who he was or what he did at Sam Heard.

He stomped in, his large gut hanging over his wrinkled pants. An equally wrinkled shirt was open at the front and his white jacket hung loosely around him.

"Hello," Mark said tentatively. He checked the chart—Gertie Fuller. "What's up?" he asked the nervous assistant, as he rifled through the file.

"That's Gertie Fuller's chart. And by the way, your memory machine is sitting in the auditorium." Forrester's chubby face sparkled with glee as if he'd personally brought the machine there himself.

"Yes, thank you, that's old news," Mark answered. "I've seen it." He sat down at the desk. "Why are you here, exactly?"

Dr. Forrester pointed to the file. "To deliver the file. Gertie Fuller. You're going to interview her, and Susan, ah, Dr. Pace, thought it would be a good idea for you to read her file first."

"Oh, she did, did she? And why didn't she bring this to me herself?"

Dr. Forrester looked abashed, lowered his head, and said nothing more. Mark watched his small, beady brown eyes dart restlessly around the office, never settling, while his narrow nose hovered over a thin, slit-like mouth that barely managed a curve when he attempted a smile.

What struck Mark the most was his skin. It was pale—overly so—as if he were anemic. It looked dry and flaky in general, and the dark circles under his eyes spoke to a life of debauchery. What was going on in this place?

Dr. Forrester began bouncing on one foot then the other. Mark eyed him. There was something about the man—nervous, unimposing, almost forgettable—that made the fact that Susan hadn't delivered the file to him personally, sting even more—perhaps a little more insulting.

"Thanks," Mark said, slamming the chart on his desk. Forrester stood army straight, tiny dots of perspiration appearing on his forehead.

"Something else?" Mark asked. He watched as Forrester ran his fingers through his thinning hair, which made the poor man's round face look even more bloated.

"No, no, sir," he stammered. "Well, yes, sort of. You know your reputation precedes you."

Mark frowned. *Was that an attempt at charm?*

The assistant continued. "We're all excited to watch you work, Dr. Moore." Still Mark didn't respond, waiting patiently for Forrester to leave. "Just so you know, we do have two other patients who might be appropriate for your machine. I mean, if you approve them."

"Hmm. Are these Dr. Pace's patients, or are they your picks?"

"Well, Susan is my supervisor, but I did take it upon myself…"

Mark rubbed his chin as he interrupted Forrester. "Are you telling me she knows nothing about you selecting other patients for my demonstration?"

Eric wiped away a bead of perspiration. "Oh, she might be angry at first, but honestly I think she'll also be relieved someone else made the selection for her."

"How so?"

"She's been obsessing about it all week—saying if the machine actually works, her entire career could be discredited. That she might lose her job…might have to leave town. I tried to reassure her. She's rattled."

Mark's chest tightened. Why? Is she in trouble?

"It was the barn fire two years ago. See, now the cops think it might be arson," Forrester blurted. "Arson is almost impossible to prove, but I think the cops are still interested in what Dr. Pace or her mother or sister might know." Forrester began bouncing again, lightly, from one foot to the other again, unable to make eye contact.

Eric Forrester was definitely hiding something, but for now, Mark decided to chalk it up to nerves or being uncomfortable meeting a superior. He had to keep his focus on the machine.

"Susan's an incredible doctor," Forrester said, struggling to keep his composure.

Before Mark could answer, Forrester continued.

"Look, I'm not really at liberty to reveal confidences, but she's had quite a bit of personal drama recently."

"Yes, she told me about her mother," Mark answered patiently.

Forrester moved closer to the desk. "No, I meant her…boyfriend."

Mark slammed his hands on his desk, rising, glaring at the man in front of him. "Is there anything else, Eric?" He'd already heard most of the story. He just wanted this gossipy man out of his office.

"Um…" Dr. Forrester proffered a yellow lined tablet with names on it. "Okay, well, here's the names of the two other patients with dementia, so you can meet them all and make up your mind which ones are appropriate for your machine."

Forrester turned and opened the door, clearly eager to make his exit. But then he paused, glancing back over his shoulder.

"Has anyone taken you around yet? Shown you the grounds, introduced you to the staff?" He hesitated, then added, "Especially now that Dr. Dennis is gone…in such a horrific way." He gave a quick shake of his head, as if trying to erase the image.

Mark took a moment, then said, "I am curious about the burned-out barn. What can you tell me about that?"

The air in the room shifted—subtly, but unmistakably. It thinned, heavy with something unspoken, as a hush settled over the mood like a warning.

Forrester's face tightened, and his hand twitched, almost imperceptibly. His expression went flat, guarded. He stopped hopping from one foot to the other as if a line had just been drawn.

"The townspeople thought that monstrosity looked

out of place in such a rural, vacation spot as Crescent Hill," Forrester mumbled. "I mean, you have to admit this city is like Lake Tahoe only without the slopes." He offered a lopsided smile, clearly unsure whether it was his place to discuss anything with the new doctor.

Mark moved around his desk and ushered Eric into the hallway.

"Well, right now, I'd appreciate it if you'd alert the staff that we are going to start the demonstration with Ms. Fuller this afternoon at three o'clock."

Forrester practically genuflected. "Of course. Yes, sure, thank you." He hobbled off, rushing toward the auditorium. Mark shook his head. What kind of researchers were they dumping out onto the general public? If he contemplated that too long, he'd get depressed.

****

Susan looked at the time. Twelve o'clock. Three hours to showtime. Oh, she didn't want to do this, but she needed to talk to Gertie before the demonstration. Before the poor old woman was subjected to memories and pain she might not have expected. "Give Mark a chance," her sister had encouraged her. "You always make snap judgments," her mother had warned before falling into the diaspora of Alzheimer's blackness.

She waited at her open office door. She had to confront him, there was no other way. She huddled inside the doorway, her arms clasping around her chest. Then his door opened, and she listened to the familiar, heavy footsteps coming toward her office.

Susan stepped into the hallway. "Mark!" she called, her voice louder than she meant, and a little too desperate.

He turned, surprised—his head lowered and looking quietly relieved. A chart was under his arm.

"Oh, good. I was just coming to see you." He pulled the file out and waving it. "Gertie Fuller's history is a little too tangled, too raw, to navigate without your insight."

They moved into her office, neither quite ready to sit. Mark crossed the room and set the file down on her desk.

"I've been going through her records," he said, voice low, measured. "Figured we should go over a few things…together."

"I think I should be the first one to interview Gertie Fuller for the machine," Susan said, cutting in before Mark could say more. Her voice was steady, her gaze locked on his. She wasn't going to flinch.

He blinked, clearly caught off guard. His fingers began tapping against the desk—quiet, rhythmic, but telling. Was he irritated? Cautious? Was he already second-guessing her?

Let him. She didn't care. At least, that's what she told herself.

She kept her tone even, businesslike. "She's seventy. Our families go way back, especially with her late husband, Harold Fuller—he was one of the original founders of this clinic. Gertie might be more comfortable if I talk to her first. You know…to ease her into the idea of participating. If it even comes to that."

She hesitated, then added, "Her family donated a fortune to memory research. But the issue is, she's not a textbook Alzheimer's patient. Most of her short-term memory's gone, but I think she has hidden memories of every detail of her life with Harold. Even if she can't access them right now, they're there. Sometimes it's like he's still alive to her."

Susan paused, waiting for some kind of reaction. A nod. A question. Anything.

But Mark said nothing.

She studied his face. Did he think she was trying to interfere? To take control? Or maybe he thought she was still running from her feelings—about the machine, about her mother…about him. Maybe she was. But this wasn't about pride. It was about trust. And right now, she needed Gertie to feel safe. Because *she* didn't yet.

And trust wasn't something she handed out easily anymore.

When still no response came, she prompted him. "Well, what do you say? Just wait until I interview her and then you can go in, is that okay?"

"Do I have a choice?" Mark stated. "Yeah, okay, you interview her, and I'll wait for your call."

****

Mark waited patiently to hear from Susan, but as the time for his demonstration drew near, the call never came. He checked his watch. An hour until show time. If Gertie had adverse reactions to being on the machine, he would lose everything he hoped to gain by coming up here. He decided to interview her. He would reason with Susan later. Perhaps this was a test, or Susan had simply forgotten to let him know when she had finished interviewing Gertie, or she might have worried that too many interviews in one day could be overstimulating. Whatever the problem was, he wasn't waiting any longer.

He stuffed his stethoscope in his pocket and marched down to Gertie's room, but when he got there,

62

she wasn't in it. He remembered Susan mentioning offhandedly that Gertie often liked to peruse the clinic's small cozy library.

Mark wandered for a while, and the small clinic was beginning to feel like a maze. He finally found the tiny library, tucked away in a cul-de-sac near the back door exit at the end of the hall.

He wanted to observe Gertie through the door's glass window before entering. He watched through the thick glass as she leaned over a large atlas spread in front of her, her arthritic fingers tracing a page in a book.

When he finally pushed the door open, Gertie sat up and smiled at him. "Dr. Moore." Her eyes twinkled.

"Gertie, you need any help?" Mark felt reenergized at her friendly greeting.

"Oh, no. Just because I finally turned seventy does not mean I'm helpless." Gertie closed the book and sat back in the ladder chair.

Mark smiled. "Fair enough. What are you looking for?"

"I was looking for a map of this area years before the clinic was built," she said. "I never knew why they picked such a gorgeous, picturesque place as this to put a dementia clinic, but Harold was always investing in different projects." She slapped the top of the closed volume. "He was trying to invest in something a few miles down the road. " She sighed. "So what can I do you for?"

Mark felt a warmth he hadn't experienced in a long time. But it was coupled with concern.

"Could it have been the burned-out barn? I thought it might just be some structure a farmer got disgusted with when Crescent Hill turned into a snow resort." She didn't respond and her demeanor didn't change, so he continued. "Gertie, you said you'd like to try my memory machine, are you at all concerned about what you might remember—that it might be upsetting?"

"No, Doctor. I want to know what I've hidden away—if I've hidden anything." The elderly woman stared down at her lap. "I have gaps in my memory and both you and Susan know that." She brightened. "Harold and I wanted to travel the world, but he was always into spending money on property. We did get to Egypt. Did you know that Abraham stood in front of the pyramids one thousand years after they'd been built?" She leaned forward.

"It sounds like you and Harold had some fascinating journeys," Mark answered.

She nodded. "We did. But you know, after he passed, I stopped dreaming of new places. Felt like the world got smaller. And I wasn't sure of my place in it."

Mark hesitated before speaking. "I'm sorry for your loss."

Gertie turned, facing him. "Thank you. That's why I'm grateful for people like you and Susan. You're going to help me remember the good times. I don't want to dwell on what happened to the barn, but I have nightmares I can't remember when I wake up and it seems the fire has consumed not only the barn, but a large part of my life. I simply can't remember everything, and now I want to. When Dr. Dennis died, I knew I had to remember more, I just had to." She clenched her hands in her lap, rubbing a thumb over the knuckles of the opposite hand. "You see, there's a desperation around here. Can't you feel it?"

Frankly, yes, he could. As Gertie became more

agitated, a shadow crossed Mark's face. If he put Gertie on the machine, could she dissociate? Would it be a strain, as it seemed to be for Mr. Rothberg? "Are you sure you want to revisit that memory?"

Gertie patted his hand. "Now you're being obsequious. Yes, absolutely I want to be on your machine."

"Such a big word for such a small lady." Mark grinned.

Gertie raised an eyebrow. "Not so small, young man."

"I meant in stature, not in intellect," he corrected himself.

"Oh, charming, too, once you let your guard down that is. Have you let your guard down with that gorgeous partner of yours?"

"I assume you're talking about Susan Pace?"

"Don't play games with me, doctor. I invented them. Listen," she leaned in so close he could smell the lavender soap on her freshly washed face. "You're a good man, Mark. But I sense a heaviness in you. Don't let past mistakes define your future."

He slowly looked at her. "It's hard to move forward when the past keeps pulling you back."

"Then perhaps it's time to let it go," she said gently. "Forgive yourself."

Her words struck a chord. Mark felt a subtle shift within, a glimmer of hope.

"Thank you, Gertie," he whispered.

"Okay, doctor. Now, tell me—when can we get on this machine of yours?"

He grinned and explained exactly how the machine would work for her.

When he'd finished, Gertie looked at him in anticipation. "Let's go."

****

Susan checked her watch. A half hour until Gertie was to be on the machine. She couldn't explain to herself why she'd waited so long to see the old woman, but she just wanted to wait until the very last minute. Mark didn't need that much time, he was going to have the entire interview with her when she was hooked up to his memory machine.

Susan moved down the hallway with clipped, deliberate steps, each one fueled by a tangle of emotions twisting through her chest. Anger, yes—but threaded with something deeper. Confusion. Hurt. Maybe something dangerously close to humiliation. This wasn't just about protocol anymore—it was about trust. Control. Maybe even pride.

By the time she reached Gertie Fuller's door, her hands were trembling.

She opened it, expecting the fragile silence of a woman waiting to be seen, but instead—

Gertie was perched eagerly on the edge of the bed like she'd been expecting good news.

Susan took a seat beside her.

"I seem to be especially popular today," Gertie mused. "But I'm always happy for some company."

"Really? Who's visited you today?"

"Mark, my dear." Gertie turned, her eyes twinkling. "You mean he didn't tell you?"

Susan blinked. Mark had already been here? The words stopped Susan cold.

She blinked, momentarily disoriented, as if someone had swept the floor out from under her. Mark had already been here? *Spoken to Gertie?* Not like they'd planned. She opened her mouth, then shut it again.

Her mask faltered—just for a breath—and Gertie's smile twitched, as if she'd noticed.

Susan forced her shoulders back, smoothing her expression, but the crack had already appeared. And in this game, even the smallest slip could cost you everything.

"Wait, you mean Dr. Moore was in here already? I didn't realize…"

"Oh, yes," Gertie said knowingly, "and I suggest you invite him to the Alzheimer's Christmas Festival this Saturday. I'm sure he'll say 'yes.' "

Susan's chest tightened, but she let the comment slide. There was no need to convince Gertie that she and Mark were nothing more than colleagues. So, Mark couldn't be trusted. He was just like all the rest, especially her last boyfriend. Quiet like a fox, going behind her back. Maybe she courted men like that. She didn't want to sound cold or unfeeling, so she simply added, "I guess I thought Mark and I would talk with you together." Susan shook off the unexpected pain. Right now, her concern was whether the memory machine would undo all the work she'd already done with Gertie.

She turned slightly toward her patient, taking a breath before asking, "Are you comfortable being the first person on Dr. Moore's memory machine?"

"The first person? I'm delighted, honey," Gertie gushed. "When he invited me to participate, I got very excited. I know I have gaps in my memory, Susie." She leaned toward Susan. Susan tilted her head.

Gertie chuckled softly. "Look at his eyes, Susie. You'll see pain there. You can always see it in the eyes.

I used to be a witch. I swear I saw pain in his eyes—the way he holds back, afraid to let anyone get too close. But we did have a lovely chat."

Gertie placed a frail, veiny hand atop Susan's. "Don't be hard on him. Life's too short to build walls, my dear. Trust me, at my age, you realize the only regrets you have are the chances you didn't take."

The old woman began to cry softly. "I loved Harold so much."

"Oh, oh, please, Gertie, I hope you'll be able to find what you want from that machine. I didn't mean to upset you." Susan put her arms around Gertie.

Gertie wiped her eyes and was suddenly focused again. "Harold had been in the Middle East. His leg. He limped from that time forward. And I was his nurse when they transported him to California," she repeated. "We fell in love."

Susan lowered her head. "That's beautiful."

Gertie glanced at her. "Susie, don't let fear keep you from your own beautiful story. Sometimes, healing others helps us heal ourselves."

Gertie had begun humming an old tune as their session ended, something low and lilting that wrapped itself around Susan's heart like a memory. The woman's quiet wisdom resonated deeply—but it wasn't enough to quiet the fire building inside her.

****

By the time Susan stepped back into her office, her anger had fully taken hold. She was supposed to have interviewed Gertie first. That had been the plan. Mark had gone behind her back—and for what? Control? Credit? Trust clearly meant nothing to him.

She paced, fists clenched, resisting the urge to call

him right then and there. She didn't know how she was going to rein it in.

Then came the knock.

Dr. Forrester stood at her door. "It's show time," he said.

Susan waved him out of her office. The man was always inappropriate. Then she dialed her cell—and hung up. Which infuriated her even more. She didn't want to make a big fuss over it, but now her hands were clammy, and her mouth was too dry to talk. Respect. Might as well set that up now.

She punched in the number again. "Mark," she said as he answered. "That kiss—it wasn't an invitation. And it sure as hell wasn't permission to walk over me. Maybe it didn't mean much to you, but to me…" she took a deep breath, not able to tell him how much it had meant to her. "It was a mistake. A moment of weakness I don't usually allow myself. Well, look." She held the cell away from her ear for a moment. Then, "We made a deal. I asked you to let me interview Gertie first, and you agreed. So why would you go behind my back and do it anyway? Was it some kind of test? A way to remind me who's really in charge here?" She took a breath, steady but pointed. "Going forward, I'd appreciate it if you'd tell me before checking in on my patients. I'm not here to be toyed with. I'm here to work—and to be respected."

"Listen," Mark sounded short. "I waited as long as I could for you to give me the all-clear. You told me I could talk to her after you did." He paused. "And that kiss—was real."

His quick response stumped her. "Yes, I expected you to evaluate her," she interrupted him, "but I certainly wanted a head's up first. And I'll always be straightforward about my patients."

"Fine," he said curtly. "After this demonstration, let's check the other two names Forrester left on my desk, and we can work it out together?"

There was an uncomfortable pause, and Susan was sure he was checking his watch. "Okay. I'll see you in the auditorium in five minutes."

When the call ended, relief swamped Susan knowing all her patient's files were duplicated and secure in her home office filing cabinet. She could always prove who was her patient and if they were being appropriated. Beverly fell into step as she walked down the hall.

"Here we go, I guess." Beverly checked her watch.

"Oh, Bev, he went behind my back to interview Gertie Fuller. Mabel Le Triel's next. Is he going to do that with her, too?"

Beverly pursed her lips. "Well, he's…committed, that's for sure." She stopped and grabbed Susan's arm. "Sue, you know I'm loyal. Mark mentioned to me that he planned on evaluating Mabel this evening. Forrester told me Mabel's very excited about it." Beverly took a candy bar out of her purse. "Want a piece?" Susan shook her head. Beverly took a bite. "Doctors are bigger gossips than nurses, and I didn't think that was possible."

"Mark never mentioned he was going to see Mabel, either. I requested he run my patients by me first. They're my patients. Oh, Bev."

Beverly took another bite, chewing as they stepped up to the double doors of the auditorium. With a flick of her wrist, she tossed the wrapper into a nearby wastebasket, then dusted her hands together, shaking off the last of the chocolate bits.

She turned to Susan, eyes sharp with suggestion. "If I were you, I'd let him know immediately that you want to be present for all interviews."

"I told him." She practically yelled at her friend. Bev stepped back, wide-eyed.

"Tell him again, girlfriend," Bev said.

"Yes, yes, you're right." Susan's mind went back to Herman Dennis, another control freak, but this wasn't the time to be thinking about him. Still scared to confront men?

"Wait," she said to Bev. "You go in. I have to use the restroom."

Beverly shot her a suspicious glance but shrugged, pulled open one of the double doors, and disappeared into the auditorium.

Susan's stomach twisted into a tight knot. She should have told Mark when she was going to see Gertie. She waited too long to interview her patient. And thus Mark had no choice but to interview Gertie first. Was she playing games? A part of her knew she'd done it on purpose, whether she wanted to admit it or not. It would make him sit up and recognize her as a force to be reckoned with.

She exhaled sharply as she stepped into the restroom. She braced herself against sink's cool, white porcelain and met her own reflection in the mirror—pale, exhausted, and far too fragile for the battle ahead.

No. She couldn't afford to be fragile.

She closed her eyes, took a slow breath, and forced herself to pull it together. She opened her purse and took out some lip gloss, slid it on, smacked her lips together, and returned the makeup kit to her purse. That was much better. She still felt queasy. She just knew things were going to go downhill and fast. As she stepped into the hallway, she bumped into Mark walking quickly toward the closed auditorium doors.

"Great minds think alike," he quipped, then slowed down, extending an arm. "After you."

"I would have thought you were already inside."

****

Susan tugged Mark's arm just as he opened the doors. "I need to talk to you."

Mark stopped, his expression deadly serious. "I don't like the sound of that." He cocked his head inside toward their colleagues.

She ignored his comment, braced her shoulders, determination filling her face. "Look, Mark, if this demonstration with Gertie goes south," her voice tightened, "with the memory machine alone, I want to be able to jump on the stage and talk her out of…of…anything that's uncomfortable."

Mark protested, "Why now?" His voice was soft, but slightly louder. Nearby members seated in the back of the auditorium turned to look at them. "Didn't we agree, this first demonstration would be on the machine alone? To prove the machine's efficacy once and for all?" He asked, voice low but agitated. "Why are you changing the plan now?"

"Because"—she shot back a little too loudly—"it was never my plan to share. I need people to believe in my methods, too."

"And—" Mark almost yelled, but contained himself. "—I need to prove that my machine can stand on its own. I'm sick and tired of everyone treating it like some gimmick! It's time to show that it works without a crutch." He scrutinized the audience, a mix of worry and anger flaring within him. Then he called out, "Give us just one more minute, folks, please?"

Most of the spectators nodded their heads as Susan and Mark stepped out again, this time closing the doors.

They both began to speak at once.

Mark exhaled and leaned back against the wall. "Go ahead, Susan."

She didn't hesitate. "Mark, you know as well as I do that the machine has risks on its own." She crossed her arms. "Without talk therapy to guide Gertie through the memories it triggers, we could be setting her up to fail."

Mark raked a hand through his hair. "Look, this isn't just about Gertie—this is about survival."

"Your survival," Susan raised her voice, her face flushing.

"Look, if I can't prove its efficiency now, they'll close me down and I will have come up here for nothing—before I even get a chance to show what it can do. I don't have the luxury of playing it safe!"

"You mean, *we,* we don't have that luxury," Susan said in a stage whisper. "I'm in this with you, Mark, whether you want me to be or not."

Mark's expression softened. "Okay, look, give me this one time with the machine. On just this patient. Let me prove what the machine, acting alone, can do."

Dr. King trotted down the hallway, stopped at the entrance and looked at them, a strange scowl on his face. "A problem?"

"No, sir," Mark said, stepping aside as Dr. King opened the door and stared at them. "Then why aren't we all inside getting on with this demonstration?"

"Yes, sir, just give us one more minute," Susan said in a hushed voice.

"One second." Dr. King retreated into the auditorium.

Susan's eyes flashed at Mark, her voice bitter. "I'm not going to stand in your way. But this time, only, it'll just be the machine and you." She turned abruptly and entered the auditorium.

He followed, the tension still coiling in his body. Mark strode toward the stage, his long legs eating up the distance as Susan slipped away to the front row. He caught the flicker of concern in her eyes before she sat, her hands clasped tightly in her lap.

He took the stairs to the stage two at a time. But once he reached the top, a strange vertigo hit him—like standing on the deck of an eighteenth-century schooner, tossed by unpredictable waves. The theater lights blurred slightly, the air electric with something he couldn't name.

A storm was building inside him. The past. The lies. The secrets buried just beneath the surface.

Concentrate, he told himself. *Hold it together.*

But his gut said something was coming. And it had nothing to do with the weather.

Chapter Six

Mark faced the audience center stage. A cold sweat broke out on his forehead as he looked down at the staff, medical personnel, and auxiliary helpers. But his focus was on Susan.

Dr. King called up from the audience, "Doctor Moore, you're late, but we are waiting with bated breath." Of course, the Chief of Research was chiding him, but that kind of kidding recalled embarrassment and humiliation from the past. The laughter emanating from the audience felt personal.

"I'm sorry, sir, I was helping a puppy cross the street, and it threw off my timing," Mark quipped right back at him.

The audience laughed louder, lightening the strain.

"Well, let's go, let's go, let's go," the Chief barked like a coach on a football team. Mark motioned to the wings, and Rodney wheeled Gertie onto the stage.

"We're ready," Rodney announced, waving at the audience as if this were the beginning of a television reality show.

"Mrs. Fuller's ready, and she's all dressed up and very excited, aren't we?" Rodney leaned into Gertie who raised a hand.

"Don't treat me like an idiot, young man."

The audience snickered.

Rodney stepped back, his hand over his mouth in

mock regret. "Sorry, sorry, sorry." He gave the viewers a wide grin. "Break a leg."

Gertie rolled her eyes. "Don't say that, either. At this age, I just might."

Rodney marched off the stage like an actor exiting a scene and Mark cracked a smile so the audience would know it was all in good cheer. Then he moved behind the machine and began rechecking levers and buttons. Everything seemed in order, but he had to take a moment and remind himself that everything had been in order for Mr. Rothberg, too. *No, forget that. Don't think about that.* So why did his attention suddenly turn to where Susan was sitting?

"Hello, folks," Gertie called to the audience, her fidgeting making her appear anxious.

"Hi." They called back in unison.

Gertie's tiny, frail body almost disappeared in the large wheelchair, but she held herself with surprising poise, her soft, silvery hair hallowed by the overhead lights. Mark could feel the audience's excitement brewing, he saw some of them leaning forward in their seats, while others fumbled with notepads. He came around to Gertie, the anesthesia canister in his hand.

"I always numb the site where I put in the IV," he informed the audience. He sprayed the freezing anesthetic on Gertie's arm.

She watched intently. "Well, you don't need to numb my arm, doctor, I don't mind needles, I'm pain tolerant. I gave birth to an eight-pound baby."

The audience clapped.

When the sound died down, she turned to Mark as he finished anesthetizing her arm, "But thanks for your concern."

The audience chuckled.

"You're welcome." He turned to the viewers. "I believe people should be comfortable in whatever medical procedure they are undergoing." He got a strong clap for that. Satisfied, he turned to his patient. "Ready, Gertie?" he asked as he crouched beside her wheelchair.

Gertie smiled, her whole demeanor one of serenity and peace. "You bet."

He withdrew behind the machine, pressed a button. "Gertie, keep breathing nice and slow through your nose and let the breath out of your mouth."

"I know how to breathe. Been doing it all my life."

More chuckles came from the on-lookers.

Mark kept a sharp eye on Gertie. As the enzyme flowed into her system, her eyes fluttered closed. For a long moment, nothing happened.

Mark pressed another button, and the screen lit up with a picture of a beach. He looked toward the audience. Susan's hands were clasped in front of her.

"Gertie," he called gently. "Can you tell me about this picture?"

Mark pressed the button again. A picture of a younger Gertie and a handsome man at an amusement park filled the screen.

"That's Harold and me a few years after we got married."

The screen lit up with pictures. Gertie holding her son, Thomas, with Harold beaming, Gertie and Harold, and Gertie with Harold and her son. Gertie recalled them with ease, and Mark wondered if she had Alzheimer's in the truest sense of the word.

Then he pressed the button, and an image flickered onto the screen—a newly constructed barn-like building standing in a natural hollow. A wide stretch of open land separated its fresh-cut beams from the dense tree line, the woods looming behind it. The building was isolated and vulnerable—too vulnerable—a supposed hideout where damp wood carried the whisper of something unspoken, unmistakably wrong.

Gertie's eyes widened, and her voice came out breathy, seeing the picture. She sat forward in the chair, eyes glued to the screen as if taped there by some ghostly being.

"I thought they were right behind me," she whispered, panic rising in her throat. Mark checked her vitals. The monitor indicated her heart rate and breathing were in the normal ranges.

Then, like a startled doe in caught in moonlight, she added, "I thought…I thought I'd led them to safety, but when I turned around, Harold wasn't there." Gertie's lips quivered; her hands grabbed the arm rests. "I tried to buck the flames, go inside, but the fire was too hot. I couldn't get in there. I heard screaming inside, then people rushed past me without him." She began sobbing. "Except for one."

Gertie wailed, her head bobbing up and down on her chest. Mark quickly shut the machine down. The screen went black. Susan rushed up on stage as Gertie continued to moan. Mark came out from behind the curtain and knelt beside Gertie. "Do you remember who it was?" he asked as an eerie silence was punctuated by Gertie swaying back and forth so hard it looked like she would topple over.

"No, no I can't get to him," she repeated, stretching forward.

"That's enough, Mark." Susan's black eyes flashed.

She knelt on the other side of Gertie. "You're okay, Gert. It's just a memory. Take in deep breaths, like this." Susan demonstrated deep breathing, in and out, slowly, deliberately.

Mark glanced over the audience and saw Dr. King squirming in his seat, a sour look on his face. The tension in the room was palpable. And Mark's anger rose. He hadn't finished calming Gertie and moving her toward a memory when Susan jumped up and began interfering. He could have handled it himself.

"Where is he?" Gertie screamed, breaking Mark's thoughts. She held her face as tears trickled through her fingers.

Susan took her hands. "Gertie," Susan urged. "It's me, Susan. You're okay, you're here with us in the auditorium."

Mark leaned in. Gertie looked up at him and then at Susan, searching their faces as if she didn't know them, but their appearance seemed to soothe her, and soon she began to speak in her normal voice as if she were simply narrating a distant dream.

Her eyes settled on Susan. "It was summer," Gertie said, now telling a story. "I can still feel the warmth of the sun on my skin. Two neighbor boys were playing in the yard, laughing, going too close to the empty barn. Ten contributors from the town had set up a meeting in that barn and their bickering was so loud it had attracted the kids playing in the woods. Then, all of a sudden, there was shouting. And white smoke, Susie. It billowed out of the barn, and I could smell fire. I ran to get anyone out of that place that I could." Her brow furrowed. "The boys were standing at the entrance watching in horror, and I grabbed them, pushing them behind me. It must have been a thousand degrees in there, but I still tried to go inside to get to Harold. I got in there, but by that time, the flames were spreading across the ceiling. I couldn't stay. Susie, I couldn't stay. And I watched as my husband was set on fire. Then someone shoved him out of the barn—a side entrance." Gertie collapsed in the chair, sobbing. "I ran behind the barn and watched as he burned to death!"

A hushed murmur rippled through the auditorium as the audience seemed to take in a collective breath.

Susan covered Gertie's hands with hers, and the old woman collected herself. A black monitor faced her, but she stared at it as if the image were still there. Her expression shifting from calm to confusion.

Susan looked up at Mark.

"Keep talking to her," he said, searching Susan's eyes. "You seem to have a good connection."

****

Susan felt herself soften. Compassion, not just for her patient, but for Mark, took hold of her. He understood. "She's in the middle of something important. If she dissociates, I'll need to get her medication," Susan said.

Mark nodded.

Susan glanced at the audience. All eyes seemed glued to the stage, transfixed by the unexpected drama unfolding before them. The glow of the overhead lights cast an eerie pallor over Gertie's face.

"I'm all right," Gertie called out.

Mark reached for her, concern flashing in his eyes. "Gertie, are you sure?"

"I don't want to stop," she clutched his hand, her breath coming in ragged gasps, her voice hoarse yet urgent. She stretched her free arm forward as if trying to grasp something unseen, something just beyond reach. "Harold."

Susan rubbed circles against the older woman's back and shoulder. "It's okay, Gert, just take a deep breath—"

But Gertie suddenly grabbed Susan's hands and looked deeply into her eyes. Susan's heartbeat skipped as a collective gasp swept through the auditorium. Whispers surged like a current, rising, swirling. Eyes locked on them. Breath held.

Mark's gaze snapped to hers, and for a moment, time stilled. The same alarm in her eyes flickered in his—an unspoken question, a shared fear.

Dr. Phillip King stormed the stage, his voice slicing through the tension. "This experiment is over. I'm shutting it down—now."

Mark stepped forward, cutting him off with a raised hand, his stance protective. "My client is having a breakthrough, Dr. King. Please—stand back." He turned to Gertie. "Who are you seeing?" he said gently.

Susan could barely hear him. Her breath came in shallow bursts as she tried to make sense of what had just happened. *What awful memory had been dragged from the depths? What horrifying truth had surfaced before their eyes?*

Susan turned to Mark again, her voice low, urgent. "This doesn't fit anything she's told me. Not in any of our sessions."

Mark felt the ache in his eyes. It wasn't just professional—it was personal. He needed answers. And he knew Susan could feel it—the trust between them, fragile but real, stretching tighter with every second.

Susan dropped to her knees beside Gertie, her hand finding the older woman's and gripping it tightly. Her fingers were trembling, but she held on anyway. "You're safe, Gert. I promise."

Susan sensed Mark behind her—close enough that his presence warmed her back, steadying her. And when he knelt beside her, their shoulders brushed.

For one charged moment, they didn't speak. But everything that needed to be said was in the glance they shared.

They weren't just trying to reach Gertie.

They were holding on to each other.

"She's never mentioned this much about the fire before." Susan's brow furrowed. "I would have told you. And Mark, I know I've been—difficult—but I want you to know something right now."

Mark frowned, his eyes on Susan.

"I'm proud of you. It sounds out of place, but I am. You just helped someone, someone dear to me, reveal memories that have been plaguing her. You gave her the freedom. I'm so impressed."

Mark wanted to hug her, hold her, tell her how much it meant that she'd said that, but Dr. King intervened. He moved beside Gertie. "Her body is trembling with memories so real they feel like they're happening right now," Mark explained.

"Phillip, why didn't you save Harold?" Gertie lurched toward Dr. King, as she tried to step out of the wheelchair, as if to escape a horrible fate. "The flames— they're demolishing everything." She kept reaching out to King. "Help me save him. Please, Phillip."

Dr. King shoved Gertie's hand away as Susan ran behind the curtain and returned with a glass of water. She handed it to Gertie, but the old woman dropped it, and it bounced off the stage planks, water drenching the floor. Mark knelt in front of Gertie.

"Gertie, listen to me."

The old woman's eyes rolled toward Mark.

"You couldn't have saved him no matter what you did," he said quietly. "It must have reached close to two thousand degrees at its hottest in there, Gertie. He was dead before you could do anything."

Gertie nodded, tears flooding her cheeks. "I couldn't save him," she repeated. "All I remember is a crime. And that fire was a cover-up. They said it was an accident, but I know what I saw. And there was a man there. He looked like you Phillip. You and…and…

Gertie grabbed Mark's. "You must believe me."

"We do," Mark assured her.

Susan looked perplexed as she whispered to Mark, "You must believe me, too, I would never sabotage yours or anyone's work. No one has come to claim that barn, tear it down, roll over it. We have to check the town's archives…if something was covered up, there might still be traces."

"Not in the mess I saw," Mark said. "I think we should call law enforcement right now."

Dr. King stepped between them. "I don't think that's necessary, Mark. We don't want a smear on the clinic's reputation and we're already fighting for money. I mean, is there any real physical evidence this was arson? Could it have been one of our famous storms with lightning?"

"There was no rain," Gertie barked at him. She gave Dr. King a warning stare, deeply seated in rage. "No one believed me back then. And they won't now. Everyone accused me of being confused. Well, let me explain something to you. I'm having the brightest clarity right now and I know what I saw." Her voice cracked with the weight of a decades-old fear.

"She has no idea who I am," King protested. "I probably look like someone she knew years ago."

"No! No, When the roof started caving in, he vanished—just like that." She swallowed hard, her voice breaking. "Believe me. Please, believe me."

A chill swept over Susan's skin like a warning, but she forced warmth into her voice. "Of course I believe you," she whispered, as her heart thundered in her chest as she searched the woman's face, willing her to feel safe.

Mark began to pace, the tension in his broad shoulders coiled tight. His gaze flicked between the machine and Gertie, then swept over the audience with measured calm. "All right, everyone," he said, his voice a steady anchor in the rising tide of uncertainty. "It appears the enzyme has unlocked memories we didn't anticipate—and Susan's talk therapy has helped bring them even further to the surface. Now we need to verify what's real."

Mark stepped forward, his voice firm but gracious as he addressed the audience that was still left. "We'll notify you when the next demonstration is scheduled. Thank you all for coming."

Confusion rippled through the crowd, low murmurs passing from row to row like a tide of doubt. A hesitant smattering of applause followed as the audience rose and trickled out, conversations hushed and uneasy.

Susan's heart still racing, Mark's eyes met hers across the room—steady, sure—and in that moment, she felt it.

Gratitude. Trust. And something more dangerous than either.

Hope.

****

From the wings, Dr. King gave a silent nod. Rodney appeared beside him, guiding a wheelchair onto the stage. He helped Gertie into it with surprising tenderness.

Without a single word to Mark or Susan, Dr. King turned and pushed through the double doors, his white coat billowing behind him like a ghost vanishing down a corridor.

Susan straightened slowly, watching him go.

Mark moved to her side, his voice low. "Was that weird?"

"What—that Dr. King ghosted out without so much as a grunt?" She shrugged, but there was tension in her smile. "Not really. He's always been strange. Detached."

They stepped through the wings together, the hush of backstage returning, broken only by the fading echo of footsteps and distant hallway sounds. As they walked side by side down the corridor leading to the patient rooms, Mark glanced over at her.

"He didn't like what Gertie remembered."

"No," Susan murmured. "He didn't. And if I'm right…he has a very good reason to be afraid."

Susan's gaze couldn't leave Mark's. Backstage she grabbed him and leaned against the wall. They could hear the applause from a few stragglers in the auditorium. It was hesitant, awkward, and short-lived. As the lights dimmed and murmurs swirled through the theater, Susan could feel her pulse still racing.

In the darkness of the theater wings, the hush was deeper, almost sacred. Everything felt suspended—like the world hadn't quite caught up with what had just happened.

Susan pressed a hand to her chest, trying to slow the pounding there.

"Susan."

His face shadowed, eyes locked on hers like she was the only steady thing left in a world unraveling at the edges.

"Are you okay?" His voice was low, rough around the edges.

He didn't wait for her answer.

His hands lifted—one brushing her arm, the other hovering near her cheek, then dropping away like he didn't trust himself to touch her.

He hesitated. "The man she saw—"

"Still out there," she finished, her voice trembling. The darkness was cut by sharp lights above, but their eyes held, the air thick between them.

Mark's jaw tightened. "I didn't expect this. Not today. Not like that." He raked a hand through his hair, the gesture that appeared to be filled with frustration, fear…and something else. "When she said she saw someone in the fire, I-I watched you. I could see what it did to you."

Susan swallowed hard. "Because I believed her. And Harold and my father, Walter Pace, were best friends."

"I know you believed her." His voice softened, deepened. "That's what makes you incredible. Are you saying your father was the ghost?"

"No, Mark, but Daddy must have been around there." She buried her face in his chest. His words hit her harder than she expected.

"I couldn't have done it without you here," she said quietly, her throat thick. "When everything went sideways, you didn't flinch. You...you looked at me like you still trusted me."

"I do."

He said it without hesitation.

Then silence again—electric, pulsing. He stepped closer, close enough that she could feel the warmth of his body through the thin space between them.

"If we're not careful," he murmured, his voice almost a whisper, "this thing between us is going to complicate everything."

Susan's breath caught. "You say that like it hasn't already."

For a moment, neither of them moved. Then his hand lifted, slowly, giving her time to pull away.

She didn't.

His palm touched her cheek, warm and steady. She leaned into it before she could think better of it.

But just as his mouth neared hers, a door slammed somewhere down the hall and Susan startled. The moment shattered—but not lost.

Mark took a step back, his eyes still locked on hers. "We'll finish this later."

Susan inhaled deeply to slow her racing heartbeat and said in a harsh whisper, "I'll hold you to that."

And she meant it.

****

A fire burned in his chest—not anger, but something sharper, more relentless. His memory machine was only a piece of the puzzle. Whatever had happened at the barn ran deeper—fraud, theft, maybe even murder. And for the first time in a long while, he felt the rush of purpose, the thrill of chasing the truth. He wasn't just a scientist anymore. He was a man on the verge of uncovering a conspiracy that had stayed buried for far too long.

Susan's voice cut through his thoughts. "Mark, your machine is not just for dementia therapy, it's got other possibilities. Possibly even in criminal investigations. I think it's our duty to explore that further."

Mark followed her as they went back to her office, his pulse quickening. He wasn't just following her—he was lost in thought, searching for the right words, the right way to talk to her about what just happened between them and Gertie's memory.

"If this is what the memory machine can do," he began, his voice intense as he shut the door behind them. "So what we're both saying, I think, is the machine has capabilities beyond helping people remember. It's about healing. I'm not talking only about what our work will do for patients. I'm talking about us. About what we could build—here, together."

Susan sat in a visitor chair facing her desk, her head in her hands. "Mark, I-I can't even believe what I saw today. I hear you, I do, and I even agree, okay? It's just we're in something really deep. I think you're right, we should call the cops."

"Like King said, we don't have any real evidence of foul play. If there was a suspicious fire, there must be records of the blaze—arson investigators, police reports, fire department logs. Suspicion of a cover up. Where did all that go?" Mark leaned against the wall. "I mean, what really happened that day?"

"You deserve a congratulations, Mark. That's what I'm focusing on."

Mark watched her face change, and her expression

turn to one of warning. "Mark, if there's any truth to Gertie's story, this town may have buried a secret long ago. And we might be the only ones who can uncover it. And you're right, I think we just accomplished the thing we both wanted." When Mark didn't answer, she added, "Well, we sure got more than we bargained for."

Chapter Seven

Later that evening, as storm clouds thickened overhead, Susan moved through the clinic with quiet purpose. Her first stop was Gertie's room. She stirred at Susan's touch, her head bobbing slightly as her eyes fluttered open, unfocused and searching.

"I-I feel a lightness I've never felt," Gertie said softly. "I remember it all now. And I'm not afraid anymore. It's like…it's like I can finally let it go."

"It was two years ago," Susan reminded her. "But remember, post-traumatic stress can come for any harrowing event, and we can forget important facts surrounding it."

"But not one so important." Gertie pounded the sheets with tiny fists, then leaned forward conspiratorially. "Harold took money to build the clinic and trusted it to someone on the board, but the money disappeared." She sighed. "Susie, I dreamed about him. I've hidden the whole nasty affair from my memory because I couldn't stand to remember it."

Susan fluffed her pillow. "We're supposed to debrief clients who do any experiment, you know. So I'm here to debrief you."

"Forget it, honey, I'm debriefed. I'm relieved, Susie."

Suddenly, an expression of wonder crossed Gertie's face. "Carolers. Hear them? Is it Christmas time already?

Again? I need to buy you something wonderful."

"It's enough to have you as my patient. That's my present," Susan assured her.

"You're the only one I can trust now." Gertie leaned into Susan, her expression secretive. "Mabel isn't doing well. Her memory is going fast. You know we spent time in that nursing home together and then I came over here and she followed me. But now she holds a secret, too. Someone in the nursing home became her lover. Can you imagine? And at our age? Goodness."

"Get some sleep now, and if you need me, press the button here, promise?"

"Yes, yes, of course."

The door opened quietly, and Mark walked in, a file tucked under his arm. Gertie sat up. "No, doctor, I can't do it again."

"You don't have to," Mark said. A dark, five o'clock shadow had appeared on his chin and his green eyes were red-rimmed, but Susan found it exciting. He seemed more relaxed.

"I've called the cops," he announced. "A Jaime McPherson answered."

"Yes, he's the only detective here in Crescent Hill," Susan said.

"Good for you, doctor," Gertie said.

"He wants to see us tomorrow at the station." He came over to Gertie and picked up her hand. "You've faced your demons, Gertie," Mark said.

"Yes." Gertie lay back on her pillow. She faced the ceiling, mumbling as if talking out loud into space. "No one here is safe as long as those dirty dogs are out there pocketing money and thinking we're going to reveal who they are—" Gertie sat upright. "—Until today, I honestly couldn't remember it all, much less speak of it out loud."

"But you did." Mark said. "And we're going to make sure you stay safe."

For the first time since Mark's arrival at Sam Heard Clinic, Susan saw confidence in his eyes. She just hoped they all wouldn't pay the ultimate price for it.

Susan wasn't so sure how accurate Gertie's memories were. When they reconvened in his office, she found herself checking over the figures that he had spread out. As far as she was concerned, Gertie's session had been both a breakthrough and a troubling revelation. She watched Mark's fingers absently trace the edge of one of the machine's logs, his brow furrowed.

"There's something else we hadn't considered." He didn't face her. He concentrated on the outline of the study. "Susan, what if Gertie's memory has nothing to do with the success of my machine and everything to do with advanced age? With filling in memories?"

Susan sat forward. "We agreed that could be a possibility, but I think the question is, what exactly did she remember and how accurate is it?" Her dark eyes burned with intensity, as if she were grasping at the thought that this demonstration could have been a fabrication to make sense of a terrible tragedy.

"Mark—Gertie was so calm when she first described the fire, then she suddenly started screaming in panic about losing Harold."

Mark thumbed through a file. "I think she knows who this ghost is and is still too traumatized to tell us." He stepped up to the filing cabinet and peeking under the desk, came out with a bottle of water, which he opened and poured into the coffee maker. In a few moments a delightful rich smell filled the room as dark coffee spilled into the carafe.

"I need something stronger than coffee," he said.

"Well, you have an entire bar at your disposal." A mock sadness covered her face.

"Okay, okay. I haven't had time to redecorate." Mark smirked and grabbed an expensive bottle of unopened Scotch. "A little fortification." He held it out. A silent offering.

Susan nodded. He poured a splash into her cup, the rich aroma curling between them. She settled in her chair, and they sipped in companionable silence, the weight of unspoken thoughts hanging in the air. Then, a knowing smile spread across her lips.

"Mmm, wonderful. I think I love you," she said, an elfish grin crossing her face. Then realizing what she'd said, "Oh, I'm sorry." She began gulping the drink too fast and brushed off driblets with her sleeve. "Look at me. So elegant." Then, shaking her head, she added, "I'm a terrible, sloppy drinker, Mark." She burst into laughter.

Mark shot her a surprised look, and she lowered her head. "Thank you, for the laugh. I needed it," he said.

She took another sip before carefully setting the glass down on the blotter. She folded her hands in front of her, her eyes locking onto his with unwavering intensity.

"Mark, I want to settle something right now. I don't usually discuss my personal life." Susan's gaze followed Mark as he set his drink down and sat behind his desk, unconsciously mirroring her posture.

"Susan, I think we're getting a little tipsy, and despite that, believe me, I respect your position here, and I'm happy that both of us are involved in this. It strengthens the studies and just may keep this place open."

His voice softened, a clear attempt to smooth over the tension that had crept into the room. Yet, beneath his words, Susan still felt it—that quiet, electric pull between them. It flickered just beneath the surface, an unspoken spark neither of them seemed ready to acknowledge, yet neither was willing to extinguish.

Susan kept her eyes on his, but the light in them dimmed as it appeared she was reaching for her drink. Instead, she grabbed a file off his desk and put it in her lap. "Okay," she said, rifling through it.

"Wait a minute. Wait a minute." Mark stood. "We haven't finished the last bit." He burped slightly. "Excuse me." She giggled, and laughter erupted from his mouth. "I have no intention of flirting with you or being unprofessional. Just so you know. My lifeline is on that machine and if it fails me again, I'm through."

"And if it succeeds, I could be through, also." Susan shot her gaze toward him. "Together we can both be successful. Or together we could both go down in a blaze." She put the file back on the desk. "Okay, just as long as you know we're both focused on this work, and the patients."

"I don't think that was quite the right analogy, that bit of going down in a blaze," he said, putting both hands up in surrender.

Susan muffled a burp. "I guess not.

Mark stood, moved to the percolator and poured himself a cup, then opened his file drawer and took out a creamer and some sugar. He dumped two packets of sugar and too much cream into the coffee and began drinking.

"Guess it's time I sobered up," he murmured, eyes

locked on hers. "Because whatever this is…it's starting to feel dangerous. And I don't want to mess it up."

"Would you like to give me the name of your cardiologist just in case the booze, the coffee with too much sugar, and the cream give you a major heart attack?" She giggled, her black hair spilling over her shoulders.

"You're no one to talk," he said. "The donut box at the reception desk that somebody left for Christmas for the staff was empty this morning and I figured Bev hadn't eaten them all."

Susan's eyes widened. "Oh, you think it was me?"

"Well, you are her best friend, aren't you?" Mark smiled.

And Susan couldn't help herself. A grin formed on her lips as she watched Mark put the cream container back in the file drawer. "Stop, stop. I'm sorry, Mark. That cream needs to be in the refrigerator. It'll get sour."

"What? I just stole it. You want me to take it back now?"

"No. Later. I don't know. We're getting silly. Probably because we're so stressed. And probably, because I'm excited to be included in your study. I *am* included, right?"

"Yes, yes, of course, you are," he answered, but the frown marks on his face made Susan doubt.

Mark watched her in silence as she drank the rest of her drink. When she put the cup down again, she looked at him. "Dr. Dennis said the MRI showed Gertie's ventricles were enlarged, indicating old age and possibly beginning dementia. Your machine may be doing a lot more than retrieving memories, what if it's also reshaping them? What if it's giving patients an edited version of what really happened to them?"

"No, no that's not possible. It wasn't designed to do that." Mark stirred his coffee and took long sips. "That's not how I built it. The enzyme is supposed to replace the one that was depleted. That's it. The enzyme doesn't alter memories, it helps retrieve them. It accesses the mind's archives, finds what's there," he repeated. As if trying to convince himself.

"But how can we be sure of that?" Susan countered, her voice steady but urgent. "The brain doesn't store memories like a hard drive. Memories change every time we recall them. What if the machine is amplifying that process? Making that feeling of 'fight or flight' so intense that the memories change in order to accommodate it?"

****

Mark could feel his excitement escalating as he sensed her commitment to his work. He ran a hand through his hair, contemplating the weight of her words. He was convinced the machine could only retrieve true memories, not create new versions of them, or change them.

"Besides talking to Jaime McPherson, what else do you suggest we do?" he asked.

"What every good scientist does. Replicate the experiment. You know from your graduate studies that every experiment must be replicated with similar conditions and similar patients in order to be verified in any way." Susan's fingers played with the edge of the blotter. She sat back and folded her fingers across her stomach. "Let's move on to Mabel Le Triel. Put her on the machine, introduce the enzyme, use pictures, then let me turn on some music, or better yet, listen to piano concertos, then talk." She looked up at him, determination in her gaze. "If the machine is altering her memories, then that's proof we need something to anchor them to reality," she said, hope in her eyes.

"But how would we know the memories are being altered?"

"By asking the same questions multiple times. And checking out what she says with what is documented in her files. Repetition will, in itself, correct any misremembering. Don't you think?" Susan asked, frowning.

Mark said. "Okay. Go on."

"First, we know Mabel's history. She was a dancer, a singer." Susan paused. "So, *after* the enzyme does its work, let me show her old photographs from her past life, her youth while she's hooked up to the machine and if she identifies them over and over again with the same memories, that should be tangible evidence the memory is solid. My talk therapy can help her process what she's seeing and recalling."

"Dr. Dennis didn't think we could rely on talk therapy. He dismissed the scandal in San Francisco, thought they were based on lies."

A woeful expression crossed Susan's face at his words.

Mark shook his head—"I think his motives had nothing to do with helping the patients. I think he wanted to deflect attention away from the burned barn—? So, what if he had people focus on getting money for an innovative treatment, not caring if it worked or not. What if he helped swindle Gertie's husband? He wouldn't want the investigation to continue. The town would be fascinated by a 'magic' machine as you and he probably called it, and they would forget about the fire."

Susan stared at him. "Oh, Mark. I just can't believe it. His death was ruled an accident, but what if?"

He watched her struggling, but kept silent, waiting for her to finish.

"I'm afraid you might be right. He did want to make the powers that be invest in something new—anything new."

A shadow crossed Mark's face, his remorse unmistakable. He let out a slow breath. "That's why he didn't care that I'd been fired in San Francisco." His voice edged with regret. "He didn't want to know the truth. He wanted to deflect a crime."

"Don't run yourself down. We're not sure it was a crime. And the only proof we have is Gertie's memory." Susan came over to him and sat on the edge of his desk. "You have a brilliant idea here, and you have a brilliant mind, and Herman wasn't wrong in wanting to move forward."

"I think so, too, but his objective in getting me up here was a slight of hand. If my machine could be shown to be any good at all, people would reinvest in the out-patient clinic."

Susan rubbed her face with both hands. "Yes, if Dr. Dennis could show the board, and the government grant people, that we were adding to the talk therapy, that would have kept the clinic viable." Susan's voice softened. "I've always believed that memory is emotional and subjective. Maybe the machine is too powerful to be used on its own. Maybe it needs to be paired with something that can ground it."

"Another thought came to me." Mark lowered his voice, slowing his words as he steepled his hands in front of his face.

"What?

"It's possible that Dr. Dennis wanted unconsciously to expose the whole operation. You loved him. He must have been a decent man, and this didn't sit well with him." He looked into Susan's eyes. "So, we have to ask ourselves, did Dr. Dennis die from an accident or was he killed because he was going to reveal the theft?"

Susan nodded. "We need to find 'the ghost.' "

"My Aunt Jenny would have loved this," he mused. He took an old rusted-framed picture of a woman standing in front of an eighteenth-century house, holding a little boy's hand and offered it to Susan. "Meet my Aunt Jenny. She would have approved of you. She was my greatest champion. She warned me against trusting Angela, and I wondered how she knew."

Susan took the photo and studied it. "You look so happy, Mark. She must have been a lovely person. I'm sorry I didn't get to meet her."

She handed him the picture. "So Angela's the person who has put the reins on you being able to commit?"

The tension that had filled the room escalated. Mark didn't answer.

"I told you my story. Now you need to tell me about Angela. Is she the person that's made you so uneasy about commitment?" She seemed to be standing her ground.

Mark gave a soft, slightly drunken laugh. "She's why I left San Francisco."

"She stole your research?"

"Not just the research. I know I wasn't exactly forthcoming about why I left. Sure, the machine had a lot to do with it, and my reputation was damaged, ruined actually, but Angela was the real reason I didn't stay and fight."

Mark sat quietly for a moment. "She loved to create problems," he said, now that he thought back on it. "I'd mention a great idea, and she'd push me forward to start it because she was never sure how to do research, and she knew I'd do anything for her. So, when my Aunt Jenny died, I felt alone, hopeless, and I wanted to start a new project, an Alzheimer's memory research project. Angela decided that was great.

"I found the patients, interviewed them, gathered the data and found out what they all had in common, what they didn't have in common, put it all on a computer sheet and calculated how many people could be helped by injecting them with an enzyme I discovered was missing. I thought it should be administered early or late in the disease, and I found figures that favored the earlier the entry of the enzyme, the better the patient prognosis.

"But I never got to present those figures. The next thing I knew, they had been sent to a well-respected journal, accepted, and Angela had put her name second to a man she'd been seeing all along. Another doctor at the hospital, whom she married a few months later. The journal she'd sent my info to would publish every two years, so I didn't know what damage she'd done to my work until earlier this year."

Susan sat back, her mouth open, unable to answer him. "That's horrible," she finally uttered. "Oh, Mark that's disgusting. What did you do?"

"I wrote a letter to a little known, free medical journal describing my work and my machine and how it was patented by me. And they published it the next month. That must have been when Dr. Dennis read it and called me."

"He told me that you'd add prestige to the clinic," Susan said. "That this machine was exactly what we needed to garner that grant money. But, Mark, I had no idea what a financial mess we were in."

"Yeah, I hear you. He emphasized to me that he wanted to see what my machine could do, but nothing about financial problems."

Susan stood in front of the desk and clapped her hands together. "Okay, Doctor. Well, before we get into all that, I suggest we start mapping out our new approach."

"You got it," Mark wobbled as he stood. The lingering question remained in his mind—what about the memories the two of them were creating with each other?

Susan had done her best to camouflage her excitement, but he could see through her facade. He knew she couldn't ignore the anticipation of working harder with him anymore than he could. "Personally, I think we should start with checking the police files," he said. "Let's see what Jaime McPherson has to say about the arson. Then we'll see if there are discrepancies from Gertie's memories and from Mabel Le Triel's, if she has any."

"Saturday is the Alzheimer's Christmas Festival," Susan said. "I have been told to invite you. But this is coming all from me: Will you please come to the Festival? I want you to meet as many people as possible from the town. It'll solidify your work and being here, and all that." Her eyes glowed.

Chapter Eight

Today was Friday. There was little time to waste, and Mark knew it. He searched in his file cabinet for Mabel's chart, but it wasn't there. It occurred to him that perhaps Susan had taken it, and he would retrieve it later, after he had interviewed the old woman.

He was shocked as he approached Mabel's room, seeing Eric Forrester step into the hallway, looking pleased with himself. When he saw Mark, his color changed, and his stare was challenging. Mark didn't like it. Didn't like it at all.

"What are you doing in Mabel Le Triel's room?" Mark demanded.

"Dr. King insisted I be brought into your work with the memory machine," Forrester answered. His tone was defiant. "Especially after that trial with Gertie Fuller. And I have every right to be here."

Mark clenched his jaw. What was going on behind his back? "Dr. King never mentioned it to me. Okay, fine. Then tell me—do you think Mabel's a good candidate? I see you have confiscated her file. No wonder I couldn't find it."

Forrester hesitated, flipping through the pages. "Uh…well, Susan said she'd be doing some talk and music therapy with her. And, of course, your machine."

Mark narrowed his eyes. "Did she?"

Forrester scratched his head, mumbling under his

breath.

Mark snatched the file and read the notes. Forrester stood next to him, an obedient student. Mark closed the file and held it with both hands. "Tell me, doctor. That question you have there about her birthday. Do you think demanding that a dementia patient recall the year of her birth is effective treatment?"

Forrester's cheeks burned. "I-I was getting to that."

Mark didn't buy it. He knew a fraud when he saw one. And Dr. Forrester reeked of deception.

Mark looked through the small window in the door at Mabel. Her fragile body tiny in the bed. He turned to Forrester. "Was there something specific you wanted to ask her? Something you wanted to find out before we used her on the machine?"

"No, of course not," Forrester's face contorted, and he shook his head.

"Then I think you should go back in the room and apologize," Mark said. "Make her feel more comfortable and that we actually know what we're doing."

Dr. Forrester hovered awkwardly, clearly out of his depth. Mark shot him a glance, his irritation evident. Instead of waiting for another meek response, Mark opened the door and shoved Forrester back into Mabel's room. The assistant was so flustered he didn't look like he could ask a question. Once inside, his full attention was on Mabel.

"Ms. Le Triel," he began. "You know there are a couple of more questions I'd like to ask. For instance, would you be so kind as to tell me about the music you used to dance to? I mean, what I mean is, do you remember it? The dances and music from your time on stage?"

Mabel shot a glance at Mark and rolled her eyes. Then her face softened at the mention of music, and she nodded slowly. "Yes…of course I remember. We danced to Benny Goodman. 'Sing, Sing, Sing' was one of the songs we danced to. And then, of course, there was oh my, oh my. I remember '*Lili Marlene*.' "

She began to hum and then raised her arms to sway with the rhythm. Suddenly, she stopped and wiped her eyes on the sheets. "Oh, look at me now. I'm all over the place."

Mark moved to the bed and laid his hand on her shoulder. "Music unlocks memories, the joy…even the ache. It's beautiful, what you're feeling."

"I've always loved everything artistic." Mabel raised her head, looked at Mark, winked. "Especially Shakespeare's Sonnets." She took a small book out of her side table and pushed it into Mark's hands, ignoring Forrester altogether. "You should read one of these to Susan. So romantic."

Forrester blushed and turned toward the door. "Well, thank you. I think we have enough."

Mark gave him a warning look, but Mabel waited for Forrester to retreat into the hallway. Then she reached out and took Mark's arm, leaning in to him. "That man's insane," she confided.

Mark handed the booklet back to Mabel. "Will you hold this for me? I need to speak to Dr. Forrester about our session on the machine." He gave her a reassuring pat and turned toward the closed door where Forrester had disappeared. As Mark stepped into the hallway, his expression darkened. He couldn't believe the incompetent assistant had lasted this long at the clinic, especially with such an inept approach to patient care.

Eric stood a few doors down the hallway and as Mark approached him, he said to Forrester, "I'm amazed you're on staff. Honestly, I'm starting to wonder if you even went to medical school."

The assistant's shoulder fell, utterly defeated. Mark forgot the man as he turned away, his focus now on how he could help Mabel, without Forrester's interference.

****

Susan took hot cocoa into Mabel. She knew it wouldn't be easy working with her. The older woman was not an Alzheimer's patient, not in the true sense of the word, and worse, she also lived a good deal in fantasy. She just didn't have the tell-tale signs of Alzheimer's such as losing track of who in her family was still alive. When Susan entered the room, Mabel turned abruptly and tried to lower the guardrails, Susan hurried over to her, careful not to spill the drinks as Mabel squiggled uneasily in bed, her usual vibrant energy subdued.

"Oh, goodie. I thought you were that horrible little man who came in here before Dr. Moore. Forrest or something," she told Susan.

"No, just me." Susan put the cup on the bed table. "But hold it, tiger. Would you like to sit up?"

Mabel nodded and Susan loosened the rails and helped the old woman off the bed and into a visitor's chair.

"I brought you some hot cocoa." Susan handed the drink to Mabel carefully.

"You are so sweet, honey," she said, then whispered, "I got a secret, Susan."

Susan took a sip of her drink, not quite sure how to answer that, but found it amusing, nonetheless.

"All my life, I've been the star, the one who brings joy to others," Mabel said, holding the mug with both hands and resting it in her lap. "But sometimes, I have to face it, the spotlight's faded, and the silence haunts me. In the nursing home, I got a lover. I'm serious. Don't believe me, that's fine." She searched Susan's face.

"I believe you," Susan smiled and drank a little cocoa.

"I thought everybody knew. But they didn't and when I moved here, sure enough, my lover followed me, and we've only been together a few months." She sipped the cocoa while keeping a sharp eye on Susan. "I thought everyone knew when my birthday was, too, for goodness sake."

Susan frowned and reached out. "Of course, everyone here knows when your birthday is. You're a day before Christmas. How could they forget. And we all pitched in to get you something special."

"You didn't?" Mabel looked stunned. "It's a week away."

Susan put a gentle hand over Mabel's. "You've got legions of fans. Everyone who's ever been to the Follies knows who you are. And we're all here for you."

"You're sweet, dear. But it's not the same as having someone to share your life with. I chose the stage over love, and while I don't regret my career, I do wonder what might have been." She leaned into Susan, conspiratorially. "I found—" She looked around the room in mock worry that someone might overhear them. "—My secret love, too late. Just like the lyrics in that old song."

Susan considered what she wanted to say next, but instead smiled at her patient and took another sip.

Sometimes being quiet was better.

Mabel frowned. "The Alzheimer Christmas Festival is starting, if I remember."

"Yes, that's right," Susan sighed. "Oh, not you, too. Yes, I invited him."

"Gertie's coming, too. This is going to be a wonderful gossip fest." Mabel's face lit up as she finished her cocoa and handed the cup to Susan. "Ready to get into bed," she announced.

Susan swallowed, took the cups, and placed them on the side table. "And Mabel, you know what? You're scheduled to be on the machine on Monday. How does that sound?"

"It sounds perfect." Mabel leaned over, coughing and sputtering. Susan rushed into the bathroom and came back with a glass of cold water.

Susan handed the cup to Mable and helped her balance it while she drank a few sips of water. "I think you're getting too excited. Here drink this and we're going to calm down."

"Just so I don't have to deal with that awful little man," Mabel said, lifting herself into the bed.

"That's okay," Susan reassured her. "Monday. But tomorrow is Saturday, and I promise it'll be just Mark and me at the festival. We're looking forward to it."

Chapter Nine

The weekend had arrived, and Mark parked his motorcycle just outside the grand entrance where a huge banner overhead announced, "Alzheimer's Christmas Festival." He removed his helmet, breathed in icy air, and then took in the bright, happy sights around him. He could hardly wait to see Susan.

At last, a fun, quiet, and contemplative event where he didn't have his stomach in knots. He pulled his guitar out of the backseat basket and slung it around his shoulder, then grabbed the large brown bag of pastries he'd stopped off to buy at Helmut's, and stepped through a newly constructed arch which connected both sides of the street. A masterpiece of festive cheer. Lush green leaves and gleaming shiny, red, yellow, blue, and silver Christmas balls adorned it, interwoven with shimmering loops of cascading silver tinsel.

The atmosphere immediately transported him into a magical wonderland. Kiosks lined both sides of Main Street, taking up the entire block, which amounted to twelve well-stocked, individual stalls that held puzzles, games, food, drink, even card games. Just as he stopped at the first kiosk, an ornamented train took off on railway tracks that led into a dark tunnel. "Just a kid at heart," a familiar voice said. He turned and was face-to-face with Susan, her black eyes reflecting the lights around them.

She looked like a storybook princess, draped in

layers of crinkly lace and taffeta that rustled softly with every movement. A delicate tiara with large, shimmering rhinestones perched atop her head, catching the glow of her glossy black hair, which cascaded in soft waves down her back.

"I didn't know this was a costume party," Mark quipped.

She pushed him lightly. "It isn't. I'm just getting into the spirit of the season."

"I should have come as an elf," he answered.

"You are an elf," she said. The golden hues of the ornaments shimmering across her face made her look ethereal.

Mark's breath hitched. He had always thought Susan was beautiful, but tonight, she was breathtaking. The soft glow of the holiday lights cast flickering reflections in her dark, gorgeous eyes. For a moment, he forgot about everything—the past, the pain, even the plan forming in his mind. There was only her, standing before him like a vision spun from dreams. A slow smile spread across his lips, his chest tightening with a rush of emotions he hadn't dared to name before. "You look…" His voice faltered, rough with feeling. "Like magic." His heart beat so hard he thought she might hear it.

She took the bag of pastries he held in his hands like a kid bringing a present to a birthday party, her eyes still on him. "Very, very kind of you. Thank you."

Mark didn't hear a word she said. He was drowning in her—she was warmth and temptation wrapped in one, a siren in winter's chill. His pulse stumbled, and as he shifted his weight, his hand brushed the edge of a kiosk counter.

A delicate ornament wobbled.

He lunged, catching it before it crashed and scattered into a thousand glittering shards. Relief exhaled through him—until he heard her giggle, low and teasing, full of knowing. The sound sent a slow, devastating heat through his veins.

"You are good at catching things," she quipped.

Mark set the ornament back carefully, but the damage had already been done. Not to the glass bauble—but to him.

Susan Pace was going to be the end of him.

Susan took his hand and walked him to the next kiosk, where three cheerful vendors poured a concoction of something that tasted like fruit juice, but laced with something a lot stronger.

"Come on, let's see everything they're offering this year." Susan took a sip, then set the cup on a counter and, like a child, pulled him down the street.

Mark looked around. The entire town had come together for this annual event, with shopkeepers, families, and volunteers throwing themselves into the festivities. The air was thick with the scent of roasted chestnuts and cinnamon.

Susan opened the bag and pulled out a cream donut.

"Oh, I see you've endeared yourself to Helmut's Donut Delights."

"Ever since someone gobbled them down in the breakroom, I've wondered where they came from. Now I know," Mark said. "The staff was very friendly."

Susan squinted. "Oh, I'll just bet. I don't blame them." She searched through the bag. "After you probably bought out the store."

"The aroma enveloped me. Kind of like right now with whatever perfume you're wearing."

Susan laughed. "Did you meet Bella? Dazzling smile, blonde hair, a little too over the top. She probably took charge and put every donut they make in here."

Mark stopped short. "Meow," he said.

"Oh, I'm being catty?" Susan pushed her head into his arm lightly, then studied the bag's contents. "Oh me oh my, it looks like she even meticulously wrapped the cream donuts separately from the glazed ones." She stopped. "Holy cow, what did you charm her with? Bella never puts cinnamon rolls, strudels, cream puffs, and madeleines in the same bag."

She stared at Mark in mock astonishment.

"We wouldn't want the cream from the donuts ruining these Danish cakes," he said with a wink, pulling one out and taking a large bite. She rubbed a small spot of cream off his cheek with her thumb. He took her hand and Susan moved backward slightly, her face flushing.

"You're terrible," she said and turned to the first kiosk where Beverly was busy arranging candy canes. "Bev, look what Mark brought?"

Bev licked her thumb. "Very generous," she said, taking the pastry bag. "I'll put them out on a tray. Thank you, Mark."

At the next kiosk, Emily Saunders, the ever-cheerful night nurse, let out a soft, lilting laugh, clinking her steaming cup of cider against Rodney's with a sparkle in her eye. Mark caught Beverly watching them with a knowing smile, her hands wrapped around her own mug for warmth. Christmas had a way of pulling hearts a little closer, he thought. And tonight, under the twinkle of fairy lights, joy shimmered in the air like freshly fallen snow. Mark took Susan's hand, and they strolled down the street, stopping at every exhibit. But his mind was on

Susan until Dr. Forrester strolled down the street toward them. He stopped when he noticed Mark watching him. The doctor, if he could be called one, turned, his face half-hidden, and appeared to browse the gifts the booth offered. When he glanced at Mark, a strange gaze crossed his face, and he turned away once more. It was almost as if he was hoping no one would notice his presence amid the bustling crowd.

Mark kept an eye on Forrester as he moved on, his attention on the kiosks, stopping to stare at photos of present and past Sam Heard patients gazing in wonderment at dolphins at the aquarium in the next county over. Mark wasn't buying his unwavering interest in dolphins. Forrester was clearly there to spy on him and Susan.

The assistant stopped at another kiosk where a banner showcasing patients engaged in weaving and painting was in full display against the back wall. Beautiful hand woven rugs were displayed along with papier-mâché figures of Christmas scenes.

A growing sense of belonging and part of the community came over Mark. Anticipation grew inside him of exposing Dr. Forrester, but for what? Seeing him now, the man was definitely hiding something.

Forrester, no longer able to try and hide, moved next to them. "Mark, I'm so glad you came! Susan." Eric's voice was overly welcoming. "A lot of important—rich people—come to these things."

"You saw me earlier, Eric," Mark answered, his eyes on Susan. Talk about trust issues. Mark could never trust that man. "How did you not stop and say 'hi'?"

He took Susan's hand and led her away.

At the kiosk down from the weaving stand, Susan's

attention was immediately drawn to Dr. King setting up a display on a white linen tablecloth. As he lifted a crystal glass, Susan grabbed it from underneath and together they placed it on the linen tablecloth. Mark was surprised. Why would Susan help King do anything, unless—unless this was a test of some kind? Convinced this change in her was a business move, he suddenly wanted to leave. He wasn't ready to risk another heartbreak, not after Angela.

"Dr. Moore, oh, Dr. Mark Moore," Beverly called from her booth where the pastry tray was now empty. She waved him over to her table. Her face lit up as he approached. "These pastries were a hit and they're all gone. You're a winner. They were fabulous. Wait, don't you dare leave." Beverly raised an eyebrow. "Oh my, oh, my. You brought your guitar. That's just wonderful! Are you going to play with Clem and Stan?" She pointed to the last kiosk where two old geezers were strumming a banjo and a ukulele.

Mark grinned, the last thing he really wanted to do, play guitar with two old-timers. What was next, chewing tobacco? "Of course," he said, pulling his guitar off his shoulder. "I guess I'll see if they'll have me."

He felt a light tap on his shoulder, and when he swung around, he was staring down at Susan, smiling broadly, her dark eyes full of excitement.

"Dr. King never comes to these things. I think we've impressed him."

"I know you have to greet people. Maybe some of them could bankroll the clinic." Mark eyed her.

Susan frowned.

"Okay, okay. I got a little jealous for a moment."

Susan took his hand and without another word they

113

strolled past the delicious scents of Moroccan, Italian, and Indian dishes wafting from the kiosks on both sides of the path. An unfamiliar warmth spread through Mark.

At the end of the kiosks, he and Susan found themselves in front of the main stage. A woman dressed in tartan stepped forward, her face lighting up in recognition. "Dr. Moore! I'm Elizabeth Johnson, Mr. Johnson's daughter," she said, shaking his hand warmly. "You helped him calm down when you first got here."

"Yes, I know. I'll never forget him." Mark reached over and shook Elizabeth's hand.

"Excuse the sugar. There were donuts in the break room at the clinic and I've been overdosing on them for a week now," Elizabeth laughed.

"So, the mystery of the donuts has been solved." Susan nudged Mark.

Elizabeth stepped forward. "I see you've brought your guitar. Are you going to play with Clem and Stan? My father loves it when music excites people to put money into the clinic."

Susan gave Mark a knowing look, the corners of her eyes crinkling with mischief.

"Of course he's going to play a song," she gushed, giving him a gentle push forward.

Mark laughed under his breath, both amused and mildly horrified. Was this really happening? One minute he was sipping cider, the next he was being volunteered for a performance he hadn't rehearsed in years. But with Susan looking at him like that—expectant, proud, maybe even a little enchanted—how could he say no?

"Ho, ho, wait a minute." Mark gave her a mock salute, then nodded and unslung his guitar. "But only if you promise not to laugh."

"Laugh? I could never laugh at you, Mark." Susan looked serious, then turned to Elizabeth. "By the way, where is your father?"

"At the clinic, I think, although about now he's probably sitting reading a Wall Street rag to see where he'll put his money on Monday." She shrugged.

Mark nodded and just as he was about to lift onto the stage to the enjoyment of Clem and Stan, Dr. King approached holding hands with a tall, model-like woman, holding the leash of a furry English sheepdog.

"Mark, Susan." He thrust the woman forward. "Please meet my wife, Annalisa, and our dog, Peppermint."

"You two lovebirds enjoying the festival? Because I hope you know everyone's whispering that you're an 'item.' " Annalisa grinned. She tugged on the leash. "Stop that, Peppermint," she scolded as the dog found a tree.

Susan quickly extricated her hand from Mark's as the two of them stared at Peppermint. "Cute dog," Susan commented, blushing but she quickly recovered. "But your intel is wrong, Mrs. King. Mark and I are working colleagues." She turned to Mark, pulling him toward the stage and nodding to the couple. "But it's good to see you." She turned to Mark. "Let's see what you've got."

Dr. King gave them a salute. "How's the study going, Mark?" He called back. It seemed like an odd, out of place question, but Mark was getting used to inappropriate behavior around this clinic.

"Fine, sir. We'll have results for you soon, I promise," he said as he lifted himself onto the planks.

King nodded and said, "Okay. Hold you to that. Last year the money was good, but we hope to double it this year." He pulled his wife down the opposite path.

A gnarled, time-weathered, overly tanned hand reached out from the stage, and Mark took it before seeing whose it was. "Welcome, young man," a silver-haired man in his late seventies, cradling a banjo, said. "Name's Clem." He smiled at Mark as the other man, smaller, wiry, with a scrappy white beard, grinned. "This here's Stan." Mark saluted Stan and watched as his nimble fingers, despite their age, warmed up with a few quick, playful notes on a ukelele. His eyes twinkled with mischief, as the two shared a glance that only lifelong friends could, the kind that said everything without a word.

Mark faced his fellow musicians, and strummed a few chords on the guitar.

And almost instantly, a crowd assembled, then quieted, as all eyes were on the trio. Mark took a deep breath, looked down at Susan beaming with a mix of pride and admiration, which made his chest tighten.

"This song is for a very special lady and for the incredible work being done at the Sam Heard Clinic," he announced, his voice steady, though his eyes never left Susan's. The two older men nodded in agreement. Mark began strumming the notes soft and melodic, filling the air with a haunting beauty. The two older men joined in with perfect harmony.

Mark sang:
Soft as a lullaby
Soft as a child
We find our hearts
By and by
Looking inside and finding the truth
And serve it to you but call it "sooth."

His fingers moved effortlessly across the strings, the melody flowing as if it had been waiting inside him all along. When he glanced at the crowd, he caught Susan's unguarded expression, her eyes glistening as if the lyrics had reached some quiet part of her. It sent a jolt through him—not pride exactly, but something deeper, a connection he hadn't expected.

When the final note rang out, the crowd erupted into applause. Susan clapped the loudest, her cheeks flushed with excitement, and for a fleeting moment, he let himself hope this performance wasn't just music to her—it was something more.

"Bravo, my fine young fellow," Mr. Johnson yelled up at the stage, behind Susan. She turned to see the dapper gentleman standing leaning on his two canes and dressed in a white shirt and black trousers, freshly ironed, his dark jacket with elbow patches and his demeanor anything but demented.

"Wow, where is Rodney?" Mark called down amid the noisy applause. "How did you get here?"

"I drove, what do you think?" He gave the canes to Elizabeth and raised his arms. "Just so everyone here knows, I'm here to support the clinic and I'm feeling so much better thanks to you and the good lady doctor." As the applause continued, Mark stepped off the stage, swinging his guitar around his back, to hold out a hand to Mr. Johnson.

"Sir, how are you this much better?" he asked as the three huddled together.

"I've been taking my medication and now, Dr. Moore, I'd like my chance at that fancy machine of yours." He grabbed both of Mark's hands. "Everybody seems to be more and more excited by it." Mr. Johnson turned to the crowd and waved as if all the exultation were for him.

"This place is getting stranger and stranger," Mark whispered to Susan as the old man began to clap. But as Mark glanced at the still-cheering crowd, a sense of satisfaction gnawed inside him. He turned to Mr. Johnson. "If you're feeling this well next week, we'll see," he said. "We'll certainly see."

Mark gently tapped Mr. Johnson's shoulder, then raised a hand to the crowd, pointing to the large glass jar set on the ground next to the stage.

"Folks, every penny goes to the Sam Heard Clinic!" he called out, his voice cutting through the noise. The crowd roared even louder, echoing across the festival.

Mr. Johnson reached into his pocket and pulled out a wad of hundreds and dumped them into the cannister. Mark watched wide-eyed. "Thank you, sir," he said.

Susan looked at him, entwining her arm in his, her eyes shining. "You are very generous. But I'd really like you to go back to the clinic. Who's here with you this afternoon?," she asked.

Mr. Johnson pointed in the direction of Gertie and Mabel. "Those two. Demanded I come."

Susan smiled at the women. "Okay then. See you back at the clinic."

Mr. Johnson nodded and moved to the kiosk where Gertie and Mabel were seated behind a counter facing each other, deep in conversation. Mr. Johnson gave Mabel as kiss on the cheek.

Susan turned to Mark. "Now wait a minute. Those two knew each other that well?"

Mark shrugged.

Susan smiled at him. "We can't figure everything

out." Then, changing the subject she whispered, "Where did you learn to play like that?"

"Why are you whispering?" A playful grin on his face.

"I'm not sure, but something very strange is happening over there." She pointed to the kiosk where the women were now pouring drinks from a large punch bowl. "I'd like to know what's in that mixture."

Susan looked askance.

Mark took her face with both his hands and gave her a kiss on the lips. She stepped away eyes wide, searching, unwavering.

"Okay. Stop that in public." She pushed her head into his arm. "So, where did you learn to play like that?"

"Isn't it obvious? My misspent youth, and my Aunt Jenny was a music teacher—many, many years ago." Mark studied her for a moment. "I'm just as surprised as you that Mr. Johnson is able to navigate and communicate like that."

"Miracles. I thought you brought them with you," Susan said as he draped his arm around her shoulders, and she felt a warmth that had nothing to do with the Christmas lights or the festive air. For the first time in a long while, she felt like she was exactly where she was meant to be—by Mark's side.

"Okay, some punch." Gertie called out as she grabbed two huge mugs and filled them with the concoction in the punch bowl. After a few sips, she suddenly burst into laughter. Mabel joined her and the two laughed until Mabel started coughing. Gertie opened a bottle of water and put both Mabel's hands around it. "Drink this before you choke to death," she said.

Mabel slurped from the bottle of water, and when

she'd finished, Gertie took out a napkin to dab Mabel's mouth.

"I don't like that cough," Susan whispered to Mark. "I want her to see a specialist."

"Acting out again, I see," Gertie said. "Stop that. This isn't the Follies."

Although their banter seemed light-hearted, Mark overheard Mabel, above the hum of conversation as she animatedly turned to Susan. "Why don't you devise a space ship that automatically transports us to an exotic island, Dr. Moore?" Mabel's tone was cheerful and mischievous. "The four of us. What do you say?"

Mark glanced at Susan to gauge her reaction. A trip? With Mabel and Gertie? He wasn't sure if the idea was charming or terrifying, but he couldn't deny the amusement tugging at the corners of his mouth. "I'd love that." Mark looked at Susan.

Susan turned quickly away, though a smile lit her face. "That sounds lovely, but I'm not sure how feasible that is."

Gertie chuckled. "Nonsense! Life is for living. Isn't that right, Mark?"

He leaned on the counter. "Absolutely. Maybe I'll devise a virtual trip machine next time."

Mabel's expression soured. "Don't denigrate what you've done, young man." She nudged Gertie who nodded her approval. "Even though a travel machine like that does sound like fun."

"You know, you two make a good team." Gertie knocked back some punch. "Ahh."

Mabel nodded emphatically. "Indeed. You know, kids, the way you collaborated—it's like watching a well-rehearsed dance. I can't wait to get on that machine of yours."

Susan's neck reddened. "We focus on what's best for our patients."

"Uh huh. Don't be so modest," Gertie chided gently. "There's more between you two than just professional respect, trust me."

Mark cleared his throat and ever so slightly pulled Susan away toward the main street.

"We're going to check out the last of the displays."

Gertie nudged Mabel and the two began exchanging knowing looks.

Mark took Susan's hand and graciously stepped away as the two older women watched.

"They're hopeless," Mabel sighed dramatically.

"Young love," Gertie agreed. "They'll figure it out eventually."

Chapter Ten

The festival was a success by every measure—smiles, applause, handshakes from grateful families, even a few donors asking about the machine. Susan had nodded, thanked them, smiled, but inside, something had started to unravel.

By the time the lights were turned off and it was time to go home, and the last guests drifted off into the snowy night, the pressure in her chest was impossible to ignore.

Too much praise.

Too many memories.

Too many reminders of Herman Dennis.

She stood alone near the exit, huddling against the cold, her breath fogging in the air. Mark stepped up beside her, silent for a moment, then gently placed a hand on her back.

"You okay?"

She nodded, but it was a lie. He saw it.

"Come back to my cabin," he said softly. "Just to warm up. We don't have to talk. Or…we can. If you want."

She hesitated. Going with him felt like a mistake. Dangerous. Because she was raw. Because she wasn't sure she could keep pretending that everything between them was strictly professional. Not after today. Not after *Gertie*. Not after Mabel's eyes filled with tears when she remembered the music she'd danced to.

But Susan also knew what was waiting for her at home: her mother locked in silence. Photos. Ghosts.

And she was so tired of ghosts.

"Okay," she said, her voice barely above a whisper. "Just for a minute."

As evening darkened the sky and Mark walked Susan back to her car, a sharp wind cut through the air. She shivered and he pulled his jacket off and put it around her shoulders. She held it tight against her body, her breath puffing out white clouds that quickly vanished into the darkness.

"But now you'll be cold." She shook under the jacket.

"Nah, got a sweater over a shirt and T-shirt." In the dim glow of the lamppost, they locked gazes.

"Did you really write those lyrics for me? On the spot?" Susan sputtered.

He squeezed her hand. "You know I did." He lowered his head, like a bashful teenager. "But I've been thinking about them for a while, so not completely spontaneous."

****

Mark's thoughts tangled. He took in a deep, icy breath and closed his eyes. He had to admit to himself her revelation about her relationship with Herman Dennis had struck a nerve, pulling emotions he wasn't ready to confront—jealousy, betrayal, and something more primal. He was questioning himself. What did he feel? Was it the pull of attraction, or was it the instinct of a savior, desperate to fix what had been broken?

Her gaze, steady and unwavering, rattled him more than he cared to admit.

"I want to make love to you, Susan," he whispered.

"And now I'm whispering because this all feels surreal. Just once, I want it to have happened."

"I want to, too, Mark. But why just once? Why do we have to quantify it?"

Her words hit him like a challenge, and he couldn't tell if it was frustration or hope that tugged at his chest. Maybe both. Maybe more.

"Maybe we don't. I'm still afraid of commitment, I guess." He took her hand. "We'll take the motorcycle. Tomorrow I'll bring you back here for your car. For just a few hours let's relax, let the clinic go, and get lost in each other."

Susan lifted her eyes to him as he led her to his bike. 'You're a poet." She sighed. Mark handed her the extra helmet he kept in the backseat basket, not for occasions like this, he told himself, but as an extra. She put it on, and as he drove them to his cabin, her arms around his waist, he could feel the shift in both of them—something unexpected.

He was afraid, even though the jacket, she could feel his heart beating too fast. Maybe it was the wind blowing off his face, or the light pinpricks of icy snow that made him think that from the moment he'd met her, Susan had drawn him in. He didn't want to admit how deeply he felt. He'd spent so long hiding his own scars, pretending they didn't exist, he'd armed himself against feeling his own brokenness. But the pull between he and Susan wasn't just attraction—it was recognition. She was like him, carrying wounds too deep to see, yet still trying so hard to ignore them and move forward.

He didn't want to keep his distance anymore.

When he parked the bike in front of the cabin, the snow had stopped, and the air was crisp. He jumped off, and without hesitation, scooped Susan into his arms. Her surprised laughter excited him even more as he kicked his door open.

"What, are you crazy?" She pulled the helmet off. "Where's the lock?"

"Door isn't locked, and it slides open on its own. I have to put books in front of it to keep it shut at night. I promise tonight I'll put a few more things in front of it. No one will be able to get in."

"And we won't be able to get out?" She laughed.

He put her down and pretended to look around furtively. She handed him the helmet, and he threw it against the hat rack.

"If anyone breaks in here tonight, they're going to get a production number you usually just see in a theater in the cheaper parts of town," he assured her.

****

"You rotter." She giggled, hugging him. She became serious again. All emotion at bay now crumbled, flooding her with feelings she hadn't experienced since Herman Dennis—only these were stronger, more intense, and ones she instinctively knew she could trust.

Susan's lips trembled; she wasn't the sharp-tongued psychiatrist who challenged him at every turn. She wasn't fighting for her place in the clinic. In that moment, she was just Susan—a woman grappling with her own past, her own mistakes.

"I didn't love him," Susan whispered. "Mark, I need to confess to you—I was naïve and stupid, but I betrayed everything I believe in. I—"

"I don't want to talk about him—ever again."

Susan nodded, as she held her breath, trying to steady her voice and bracing for what might come next.

"Okay, but now there's no secrets between us?"

Mark closed his eyes, and moved over to the couch. He sat heavily. "No secrets, no hidden agenda?"

She followed him and sat on the arm.

"I never wanted to love again." He pulled Susan down next to him. "But look, I think it's already too late."

"If she walked in here tonight, would you make love to her? I want to know."

His posture stiffened and he frowned. "It's been over between me and Angela for a long time, Susan. I knew tonight at the festival I didn't love her anymore. I think I'm falling in love with you."

She leaned into him, resting her head in the crook of his neck, and it felt as if the world outside had faded away. She couldn't explain it—why being closer to him suddenly felt like the only thing that mattered. Maybe it was the raw honesty he'd shown, or the connection they shared through their work—their mutual fight to preserve the memories of others. But deep down, she knew it was more than that.

Then, as she lifted her head, Mark stood, took her hand and silently led her up the staircase to the loft. "Susan…" he whispered, as he lowered her onto his bed, "Nothing could change the way I feel about you."

Her breath hitched, and for a moment, she was paralyzed. Then, almost hesitantly, she faced him, but before she could speak, he put a finger to her mouth. "I want you!"

He kissed her slowly and began unbuttoning her blouse as she began pulling his shirt off his shoulders. Slowly, tenderly, as if testing the waters of something new, they undressed each other, leaving clothing strewn on the floor next to the over-sized king bed. It wasn't rushed; it wasn't urgent. Instead, it was filled with the quiet understanding that had been growing between them for weeks. Their kisses deepened, and he could feel the tension melting from her as she responded, her hands rubbing his back as he pulled her closer.

He was hard against her thigh as he slid under the sheets. But he took his time, caressing her face and kissing her neck. Carefully, she let her hand touch him, then slide up his shaft until he moaned in pleasure. Oh, how she wanted to feel him inside her, but he pulled her hand up around his neck and let his lips move slowly down her chest, nibbling her breasts oh so tenderly— kissing her nipples. She stroked his hair, but she was shaking so hard with the building excitement that she clenched a strand.

He shot her look, his smile broadening, then kissing her lips again and letting his hands rub her sides. His tongue slid past her lips, then back down her neck and down toward her private parts where he let his tongue do magic that had her screaming in delight. She'd never orgasmed like that before and as she tried to pull his face up to kiss him, he slid inside her, and she couldn't move.

They came together, but after too many orgasms to count, he finally slid off her and lay back panting and perspiring, his arm under his head. Susan let her face cradle inside his arm. She placed her hand over his, her fingers tracing the lines of his palm. Their foreheads rested against each other, their breath mingling in the stillness of the room.

He pulled her to him. They lay there motionless for a long minute.

"I didn't expect this," he said.

"Neither did I," she admitted, her lips brushing against his neck. "But we don't have to fight it anymore." He kissed her. "One time, just so we can say we did it?" she mused as she tucked her head under his arm and let her hand coil the hair on his chest.

"Well, maybe we could do it again."

In a moment, he rolled over on top of her. This time, a familiar, hot love and trust seeped into Susan. Into their lovemaking.

****

Mark felt it now. His and Susan's joint efforts—years of dedication—it was all paying off along with a connection between them running richer than simple physical attraction.

But then, that tiny voice, the one that had never fully gone silent, crept forward from the back of Mark's mind. *What if I'm misreading this? What if I'm opening a door I can't close?*

When they were finally spent, his chest heaving, he turned his head toward her. "Why me, Susan? After everything, why me?"

Susan traced the features of his face with her finger. "Because you care," she said softly. "You care enough to fight for people, you are a healer, and that…that's something I am, too."

She looked at him with a tenderness he hadn't seen before, and in that moment, Mark knew. Susan wasn't just someone who challenged him professionally. She was the person who would challenge him to face his own past, his own fears. She made him want to be better, to love more fully, to heal not just others, but himself.

He pulled her closer, his heart swelling.

"We're talking too much," he said, kissing her

again, this time the world outside fading away. Mark was at peace—like maybe, just maybe, love could heal them both.

And he saw in Susan's eyes, she knew it, too.

****

It was early in the morning when Mark's cell buzzed. He stirred and looked at Susan lying on her side facing him, her eyes closed and her hand holding his as they slept.

He leaned over and grabbed his cell, checking the time. Five-thirty a.m. Nothing good happened at five-thirty in the morning. Susan stirred, the buzzing of his phone pulling her from sleep. She watched as he picked it up, rubbing his eyes, his voice groggy.

"Dr. Moore," he answered. His brow knit slightly—he stumbled to his feet. Whover was on the other end must be hysterical.

"It's Mabel Le Triel. She died," Rodney sobbed.

"What?" Mark jumped away from the bed.

"Emily just called me at home," the orderly continued. "I'm sorry to wake you up like this. I'm at the hospital now and I think you should come here immediately. Mabel left a book of sonnets for you. The little note she wrote insisted it be given to you, like right now directly into your hands."

Susan got out of bed and stood beside Mark, putting a hand on his shoulder. "What's wrong?"

Mark picked up clothes and began pulling them on, then turned to her.

"Mabel Le Triel just died. She left a book of sonnets for me."

"Good Heavens. We've got to get over there." Susan grabbed her clothes and began to dress. "Why would

Mabel die suddenly? She was fine yesterday…except for that nasty cough. Oh, I should have stopped her from doing too much. All those ballet pliés could have exhausted her."

"No, babe, this has nothing to do with you." Mark thought of the strain that might have been brought on by Forrester's visit, but his concern was on Susan. She was rushing to dress so quickly that tears ran down her face unheeded. And it looked like she would explode. He put his arm around her as they both stumbled down the staircase, hurriedly put on coats and pulled the bookcase off the front door. Outside, Susan jumped on the back of the bike, breath catching, hands trembling. Mark swung a leg over the motorcycle, started it and jammed down the road as if speed could somehow change what was happening. It couldn't. Mabel was already gone.

Rodney met them at the side of the clinic—near the service doors where ambulances sometimes pulled in. His face was pale, his voice tight, shaking, wrapped in a wool overcoat with two scarves swirled around his neck. His eyes were red with tears. "We've left her in her bed. The coroner will be here soon."

"Bev'll be devastated," the orderly continued as they moved inside and down the hallway to Mabel's room. "She loved Mabel. I know old people in nursing homes and clinics die, but we get close to them." Rodney began sobbing all over again.

Susan held him tightly, pulling him close. "Oh, Rodney, you were wonderful to her as you are to all our patients."

Emily came out of Mabel's room, tears flowing down her face. She handed the book of sonnets to Mark.

"There's a loose page in there, doctor. I didn't read

it, but it's on page fifty-one," she whispered, barely holding herself together as she walked out.

Mark watched a moment, his heart racing, then turned to the page and a slip of paper fell to the floor. He picked it up and read it, then handed it to Susan.

"This says the funds were diverted to a company and when the exchange was about to be investigated, someone torched the barn."

Mark shook the book again and a ledger fell to the floor. He picked it up. A listing bearing the company name: Agricorp Industries and it documented payments made to E. Forrester. The amounts were staggering—far beyond anything that could be explained by a physician's salary or consulting fees.

"What the hell?" Mark muttered.

Beneath the ledger, another document caught his eye: a property deed for a parcel of land once owned by the clinic. The notation read, Transferred to Agricorp Industries. Mark's pulse quickened. "Susan—" He flipped through the pages, finding a photograph of the charred remains of the barn. "—Mabel kept secrets in this diary. She knew what was going on."

The pieces fell into place. This was the evidence the barn fire wasn't a tragedy; it was a cover-up. Agricorp had purchased the land, likely at a discount, after the fire cleared away proof of environmental hazards. But how was Forrester involved?

Chapter Eleven

Mark exhaled slowly, the weight of what they had just uncovered pressing against his chest. Beside him, Susan stood rigid, her eyes locked on Mabel's lifeless form.

Rodney shifted uneasily, his hands clenched into fists at his sides.

Susan dragged a hand down her face. "Greed?" Was all she could say.

Mark's gaze flickered to the old, weathered book of sonnets and he kept turning the pages over and over. Mabel had held the secrets that had been tucked away in the ashes of a torched barn.

"Forrester is at the center of all this. Mabel literally kept a diary in this book—she knew what was going on."

Rodney let out a sharp breath. "And she paid for it."

The words settled heavily between them.

A knock at the door broke the silence. Two morgue attendants, dressed in dark uniforms, stepped inside. One was a wiry man with a clipboard, the other a woman with weary eyes.

"We're here for Mabel Le Triel," the man said, glancing between them.

"She's ready," Mark said.

Susan inhaled sharply, her breath catching on a sob she refused to release. The female morgue attendant stepped forward, unfolding a soft white sheet with reverence. As they gently covered Mabel's still form, Mark reached for Susan's hand and entwined his fingers with hers. Together they stood in silent sorrow, watching as the final veil was drawn.

The attendants moved with quiet efficiency, lifting Mabel's body onto a stretcher. As they secured her, the female attendant glanced at Susan and said, softly, "I'm sorry for your loss."

Susan swallowed hard, unable to stem the sobs. She nodded.

Rodney stepped aside as the attendants wheeled Mabel out. "Forrester isn't going to get away with this. Does he really believe no one will put the pieces together?"

"Mabel left us a trail." Mark held patted the book in his hand.

Susan took it clutched it to her chest as if it were a part of Mabel herself.

"They tried to bury the truth," she whispered. "But they didn't count on her fighting back."

Mark met her gaze. "Then let's finish what she started."

Rodney nodded, the tension in his jaw solidifying into determination. "I'm in."

"We need to get McPherson here," Mark said.

The three of them stood together in the empty room, the scent of antiseptic thick in the air. Mabel was gone, but the truth she had fought for was finally coming to light.

And they weren't about to let it die with her.

Chapter Twelve

After a long, sleepless night, Mark sat in the passenger seat as Susan drove toward the police station. The squat, single-story brick building looked like it hadn't seen a renovation in decades. Inside, the front desk was manned by a single bored-looking secretary, flipping through a paperback novel. The place was quiet—too quiet for a police department, but then again, this town probably didn't see much action after dark.

Mark and Susan stepped up to the counter. The woman brushed back a single gray hair into her tight bun and glanced up, taking in Mark's doctor's coat and Susan's determined expression. She pushed her rimless glasses up her nose. A brass name plate on her desk said, Gladys McKenzie, secretary.

"Hello, Susan. What can I do for you," she said, her face vacant of emotion.

"Gladys, we need to speak with Jaime about the barn fire," Susan said.

"He's not here yet, but you're welcome to have a seat and wait." She forced a smile. "But it's good to see you two. I've heard…good things."

Mark smirked. A small town and gossip. No way to stop it. "How long will it be?" he asked.

"Oh, he just went for a break, he should be back momentarily." Gladys grinned widely at him, then checked her 1950's style wrist watch. "Yes sireee—late lunch." Gladys looked over her glasses. "We haven't been formally introduced, but I heard you playing at the Festival. You're an excellent musician."

"He's the new researcher at the clinic, Gladys," Susan filled in. "Dr. Mark Moore. He's one of the good guys."

"Well, at least someone is." The door banged open. True to Gladys' word, police officer McPherson shuffled in. His gray-streaked hair neatly combed, though his shirt and jacket looked as if he'd pulled them out of a pile of laundry. He pushed his horn-rimmed glasses up his nose and squinted at them.

"Jaime," Gladys announced, her lips pursed, "the doctors are here to see you about the barn fire."

"How can I help you two?" Jaime shook off his coat, hung it on a free-standing rack, and plopped down in a chair opposite Gladys.

"We need to take a look at the files," Mark said.

"Why? That happened nearly two years ago."

"Murder. See, detective, this might be more about a murder than arson," Mark said.

The detective's eyes widened. "You got a warrant?"

"No, Jaime, we don't," Susan said. "But those records are public domain, aren't they?"

"Oh, you going into the law now. Medicine's boring you?"

She didn't answer, but stood defiant, looking into Jaime's eyes.

"No. Technically it's still an ongoing investigation. But only because it's you, Susan." Jaime let out a long-suffering sigh, then jerked his head toward the back of the station. "Follow me."

Gladys nodded in agreement.

Jaime led them down a dim hallway to a room lined with old metal filing cabinets. The scent of stale coffee and aging paper filled the air. Mark watched as the detective rifled through one of the drawers, eventually pulling out a thick file folder. He slapped it onto a dented metal table.

"This is a big ask." Jaime gave Susan a look that suggested he might expect a favor in return someday. "There. This is all we've got left from that mess."

"The next time your aunt needs her cough medicine, I'll sneak it out for you." Susan smiled at the detective. "No charge."

Mark pulled the file toward him and Susan and opened it. Inside were faded photographs, case reports, and handwritten notes from the original investigation.

Susan leaned in, scanning the contents. "This…this isn't just about the fire."

Jaime nodded, rubbing a hand over his stubbled jaw. "No. It's about what started it. I'll leave you two to read. Let me know if you have questions." The detective moved through the open doorway, and pulled the door closed behind him, leaving Mark and Susan alone.

After going through the pictures and reading the reports, Mark leaned back in his chair rubbing his temples. Susan still scanned the file's contents, her frustration seemed to escalate as she flipped another page.

He watched her with quiet satisfaction. He should've been focused on the case, on what he'd just read—but the feeling that he had a partner, that Susan truly understood him, stirred something deep and proud inside him. He tried to shove it aside, but it refused to go. Susan noticed him staring at her and straightened. She held her back with both hands and let out a whoosh as if her whole body had just been broken in two.

"What?" he asked.

"What?" She repeated, giving him a cross glance. "You're awfully quiet all of a sudden. If you're not going to pitch in, at least tell me what you're thinking."

He exhaled, smiled, and pinched the bridge of his nose. "Why did Gertie suddenly remember something no one else ever knew?"

Susan picked up a piece of paper and waved it at him. "She said Harold was in the barn. But Mark, Jaime's report says no one was inside the barn when it burned."

Susan leaned forward, her hands on the desk. "Look at this. More papers and statements from police here, and it looks like a bunch of stuff was redacted." She picked up another folder. "This one says Harold Fuller disappeared the night of the fire. His body was found outside and wasn't burned, someone strangled him."

Mark sat up straight. "But Gertie swore she saw him inside. That she heard him screaming."

Susan nodded. "Exactly. That detail was not in the police report. No witness, no evidence, nothing. If Harold was really inside, the town would have known. And it would be documented here. But somehow, after two years of not recalling it, the machine made her remember something that was never reported."

Mark stood, pacing the office. "So you're saying she fabricated it?"

Susan hesitated. "No, not necessarily. I think she believes it. And if she believes it, then the question is— did the machine create the memory from her fragmented memories?"

"I'd sure like to know why Gertie suddenly remembered a detail that is directly contradicted by these files."

He had no answer.

He exhaled sharply. "If the fire was ruled an accident, the investigation wouldn't have gone any further."

Susan bit her lip. "But Harold's death should have a coroner's report somewhere. If we find a death certificate, maybe there's an autopsy."

He snatched the document from Susan's hands, scanning the coroner's notes. Here's the autopsy report.

Full Name: Harold Emory Fuller

Date of Death: July 17th, 2018—Time unknown (possibly between 6:00 p.m. and 9:00 p.m.)

Cause of Death: Asphyxiation.

Location of Death: Unknown

Susan looked over his shoulder, trying to keep her voice steady. "Died outside the Crescent Hill barn fire." Mark could feel her pulse pounding as she leaned into him and took the sheet out of his hands.

Mark's hands curled into fists. "It doesn't list the barn as the place of death."

Susan pointed to the time. "But the fire didn't start until late that afternoon. Remember, those neighbor's kids were playing outside. They couldn't hear someone being strangled. Who was big enough to do that? And Harold was dead probably hours before the flames even touched the barn."

Mark's eyes darkened. "Then someone killed him, dumped his body behind the barn and torched the barn. Whoever it was, left him there, knowing the flames would probably get him, but that's pretty stupid, why didn't they just put his body in the barn?"

"Because the kids were witnesses, and they would be able to identify whoever it was," Susan said. "Someone staged the whole thing and disappeared out the back."

Mark exchanged a glance with Susan. Whatever they had stumbled into, it was bigger than he or Susan had expected.

Harold had been murdered.

And the killer is still loose.

Chapter Thirteen

Mr. Johnson had been making a fuss all afternoon, and after Mark assured him he would get him on his machine, he tried to relax in his office. He heard Susan leave her office and when he stepped into the hallway, he saw her move toward Beverly and wrap her arms around her friend. Normally, he knew she wouldn't stand around lamenting a patient's death, but this one she took hard, and Mark knew things at Sam Heard Clinic were anything but normal.

After checking over the sonnets book one more time, Mark took a few moments to tidy up his desk, and then put on his overcoat. One more look around the office to make sure he hadn't missed anything, when a sudden burst of laughter pushed past his lips. He realized he'd noticed what time Susan had slipped into the break room for an afternoon coffee and to grab one of the mini chocolate bars Beverly kept on the top left cabinet shelf. He was actually keeping tabs on her. He opened the door, but held it a moment.

Carolers had started their rounds of singing in the town and now back up at the clinic, muting the sounds in the hallway, but Mark recognized the voices. He turned off his light and opened his door partially.

Eric Forrester's voice floated down the hall, low and tense. "I can't keep doing this. I'm dizzy all the time—my legs gave out yesterday. If more money doesn't come through soon—"

"Lower your voice," Dr. King snapped. "You'll get what you need. But not if you draw attention."

A pause. Then silence.

Mark opened the door and stepped out—and both men froze.

Mark caught the tail end of King's warning glare and the guilt flashing across Eric's face.

"Everything all right?" Mark asked evenly.

"Fine," King said too quickly. "Just clinic business."

Eric gave a weak smile. "Long day."

Something about the way Eric leaned on the wall—not lazily, but for balance—set off an internal alarm. He was sick, but what was the problem?

Mark began to walk past them, but then hesitated, watching Eric one beat longer. Something was definitely up, but he didn't have the strength or wherewithal to find out what just now.

He moved past the two men quickly and reached the reception desk. As he approached, he smiled at Beverly. He wanted to be the one Susan leaned on for support, and he was chastising himself that he was still holding himself apart, immovable, just as Angela had said he would. It didn't make up for her breaking his heart, but she was right about him being compulsive.

"Looking for Susan? She's outside." Beverly winked at him.

Mark found Susan pacing outside the clinic, arms wrapped tightly around herself. The night air was sharp, but it looked like she didn't seem to notice. Her mind was clearly not on him because when she looked up, her frustration, and maybe fear, seemed scrambled into something else she wasn't ready to name. And it looked to Mark as if it was longing.

****

Susan stared at him.

After weeks of dismissing her approach, of challenging her every step, Mark had insisted that her work was just as vital as his. She should have felt victorious, but instead, she felt unmoored. Because it meant he understood her. He saw her.

And she didn't know what to do with that.

She watched as he moved toward her.

"Are you going to stand out here all night?" he asked, his voice, deep and steady.

She shook slightly, his very presence sent an involuntary shiver down her spine. He stuffed his hands into his pockets, his green eyes locked onto hers with an intensity that made her heart stutter.

"I needed air," she said, lifting her chin.

Mark stepped closer, his boots crunching against the gravel. "We handled it." A slow, knowing smile tugged at his lips.

She let out a hollow laugh. "We fight like hell, Mark. That's not exactly teamwork."

"It is when the fight makes us better." He took another step, closing the space between them. "You push me. Make me reach further. And you were right—you've been right about a lot of things."

Susan's breath caught. He was too close now, the heat radiating from him cutting through the cold. She could smell the faint hint of soap and cedarwood, the scent so distinctly him. "Mark—"

"I was afraid," he interrupted, voice quieter now. "Not just about the machine. About being here. About starting over. About you."

He exhaled sharply, running a hand through his hair. "You remind me of what I lost. Of what I wanted to be before everything fell apart. And that scares the hell out of me." His eyes locked onto hers, unguarded for the first time. "But the truth is, Susan, I never want to buck you. I just want—" He didn't finish the sentence. He didn't have to. Because she was already moving.

Before she could second-guess herself, before fear could paralyze her, she reached up, cupped his face, and pressed her lips to his.

The moment their mouths met, the tension between them shattered. His arms came around her, pulling her close, anchoring her to him. The world around them melted, the cold, the uncertainty, the walls they had so carefully built between them.

"Well, now everyone will know." Susan rested her forehead against his. "I don't know what this is," she admitted, her voice barely above a whisper.

He stood quietly for a moment, taking in what she'd said. She was quiet, too. Was she wondering what a fool he'd been, or did she understand?

"Sue, let me get it off my chest, and we can go on with our lives—see where this leads us. I'm very uncertain about whether or not I can commit to a long-term relationship. Whether or not I can love again. Angela was pregnant while I was giving her all my info. When she told me, I was certain the baby was mine. But after a DNA test confirmed it wasn't, I felt like the earth had opened under me."

Susan let out a slow breath, absorbing the weight of Mark's confession. His voice had been steady, but the rawness in his eyes told her this wound had never fully healed.

She reached for his hand, lacing her fingers through his. He stiffened at first, then relaxed—just slightly.

"Mark, you have to let the past go," she said softly. "Just like you told me to."

His jaw tightened. "It's not that simple."

"No, it's not. But it's necessary." She held his gaze, unwavering. "Angela betrayed you. Lied to you. Used you. And yet, you kept going. You kept working. You kept fighting for something real."

A humorless chuckle escaped him. "And now I'm up here, in the middle of a town where people are dropping dead and buildings are going up in flames. And now we're waiting—for what?"

"Mark, Dennis needed a fall guy." Her voice was steady, clear. "The memory machine was a camouflage."

Mark ran a hand through his hair, nodding. "And up here, away from the corporate pressure, I've actually been perfecting it." He exhaled sharply. "If Dennis needed the machine to camouflage his illegal activities, then…"

Susan squeezed his hand. "Who needed the money that badly? We need to find out who wanted that barn destroyed—and why people are dying because of it."

Mark studied her, reflecting how proud of her he felt. She was willing to fight side-by-side with him, something no one else had ever done.

Finally, he gave a small nod. "Then let's get to work."

Chapter Fourteen

Jaime McPherson sat in his station wagon, eyes fixed on Susan's house. His junior partner, Ron Morton, sat quietly in the passenger seat, chewing on a toothpick.

When Mark pulled up on his bike and cut the engine, he approached the window.

"What's going on?" he asked.

Jaime didn't look away. "Susan called a few hours ago. She sounded hysterical. Said a black van's been circling the house—hovering, then vanishing."

Mark's gaze swept the area, suddenly alert. He saw nothing.

"We can't hang around much longer," Jaime added. "We're not private security—we can't babysit every citizen who gets spooked."

"I'll take it from here," Mark said. "I'll stay for a while. Maybe overnight."

"Good." Jaime gestured toward his partner. "You know my rookie, Ron? Say hello. Kid's got a shot at detective."

Mark gave a nod. "Hi, Ron."

"Hey," Ron said, barely audible.

Mark wheeled his bike to the front of the house. Inside, Susan sat at the dining room table with her mother and Pamela, hands curled around a cold cup of tea.

"I don't know what's going on," she said, rising

quickly to meet him with a hug. "But there *was* a black van out there. Most of the day. Now it's gone."

Mark felt tension crawl up his spine. His gaze darted toward the windows—and froze. Just beyond the tree line, half-concealed beneath low-hanging branches, a large, black van sat idling.

"That's not Beverly's van," Susan whispered.

"It's too beat-up. Too…filthy." Mark didn't move, his eyes locked on the shape in the shadows. "Someone's watching us?"

Susan's voice dropped. "No. They're watching *me*."

Mark turned to her, jaw tight. "Give me a moment. I'll handle this."

"Mark—"

But Mark was already moving—fast, striding toward the van. The windows were tinted and fogged, but he approached the driver's side cautiously, heart thudding. He knocked hard on the glass.

The figure inside jumped. The vehicle's headlights flared to life, but Mark jerked the driver's side door open quickly enough that the van veered toward a tree. Dr. Phillip King fell out onto the pavement. Mark yanked him up before King could react.

"What the hell are you doing here?" Mark growled.

King's eyes darted, calculating. On the passenger seat sat a half-burned matchbook, a red gas can in the backseat. Not enough to prove intent—but enough to terrify.

Mark didn't hesitate. He dragged Dr. King toward the house.

Susan stood, wide-eyed on the porch, frozen. "Mark—what—?"

"I think he was about to torch your house."

****

Mark kicked the door shut behind them, slamming Dr. King against the wall hard enough to make a picture frame rattle.

"You're done," Mark growled, the words low and vibrating with fury. "I should let Susan have the first swing."

King tried to straighten his blazer, his arrogance flickering—but fading fast.

"Sit."

Mark shoved him into the nearest chair and yanked out his phone. "Jaime? Get here now. I've got King."

King opened his mouth—maybe to talk his way out, maybe to lie one more time—but Mark just glared at him. "Don't. Just…don't."

King struggled half-heartedly, but when he saw the look on Susan's face—he went still. Mark shoved him toward a chair while Susan locked the door behind them.

****

Susan's gaze locked on Dr. King.

"You were going to burn my house down," she said stepping closer. "With my mother in it. With me. My sister? And what if the baby were here? You are evil, Phillip."

Dr. King's smirk faltered.

"You couldn't stand that Dennis chose me, could you?" she continued. "That he was everything you pretended to be—a real doctor, a decent man, and someone who actually had my heart."

Mark stood back, letting her have the moment.

"You were never going to be him," Susan raised her voice, breaking just enough to make the truth sting. "And you knew it. That's why you tried to erase everything he ever touched."

Dr. King sank back into the chair, silent now.

Mark finally spoke. "Well. There's one more thing Dennis touched—justice. And it's about to catch up with you."

King laughed—a dry, broken sound. "This place should've gone up in flames years ago. Just like Dennis. He was an anachronism."

The front door opened again. Jaime McPherson stepped in, eyes sharp, voice steady. "We've got enough, King. With the ledger pages Mark turned over to me and Eric Forrester at the station—telling us everything you'll be put away for life."

King went still.

Susan's breath caught. "You tried to erase the clinic, erase Dennis…just to cover your own crimes?" She shook her head.

King didn't answer. But his silence said enough.

Jaime moved forward and cuffed him. "Let's go."

As he led King outside, Jaime turned to Susan. "You saved a lot of people tonight. Including yourself."

****

Susan sat heavily in the living room, her sister on the chair and Mark seated on the floor.

"We should go over all those files again," she said, but her voice lacked conviction.

Mark didn't move.

Neither did she.

The house felt smaller somehow, charged.

"You should take something and get some rest," Pamela said.

"I'm fine," Susan told her, as if trying to convince herself.

Mark reached for her hand. "You don't have to be."

Her breath hitched, just slightly. She met his gaze then—fully, finally—and something cracked open between them.

Pamela got up. "I'm going home. Call me tomorrow?"

Susan nodded, and she and Mark watched her sister go out the front door. Then Mark reached out, brushing a stray strand of hair behind her ear, letting his fingers linger a second too long.

Susan didn't pull away.

In fact, she *tilted her face toward him*, just slightly.

Mark's pulse pounded. He kissed her.

"Susan?" Susan's mother called from down the hall in her bedroom. The moment shattered.

Susan's phone buzzed. She looked at the cell's window and let out a small, frustrated breath. Mark clenched his jaw, stepping back.

"Now what?" he asked.

"Sue?" Her mother's voice sounded strained. But Susan read the message, her brows furrowing. Then, slowly, she looked up at him.

"Ma, I'm coming," she to her mother. "Mark, you're not going to believe this," she said. "But I think we just got something neither one of us nor my sister might want." Her voice barely rose above a whisper. "My father, Walter, is in town. Why or for what reason, I don't know." Unexpectedly, she thrust her face into Mark's coat and sobbed. "Why is he back here now?" she wailed.

Mark held her. "You have too many secrets and you can't keep them all," he whispered. "Just take it easy for a moment."

Mark exhaled, rubbing the back of his neck. Back to the case. Back to reality.

Susan pulled away, took Mark's hand and they went down the hall into her mother's bedroom. And there, holding a picture was Eleanor Pace. "I need to be on your machine, Dr. Mark," she stated.

Chapter Fifteen

"Look, I need to see the barn myself," Mark said as he pulled the sheets onto the couch.

"Now? This is dangerous, baby. Please, watch who's around there, okay?"

"I will." He got on the bike. He couldn't help himself. He was curious and now he knew as a scientist first and foremost he needed to look at the burned building sitting, still charred pile of rubble after all this time. He had to know what was there. It was crucial to his studies and his patients. People were hiding secrets, and he was determined to find out why.

He raced the motorcycle, the darkness closed around him, but his anticipation goaded him forward, and soon he found himself on the muddied path leading to the burned out shell of a building. It stood soggy and wet, barely holding its shape against the cold. Mark rolled the bike to a stop, taking in how out of place it looked in this calm, snowy wonderland that was Crescent Hill.

Darkness crept through the trees, and his mind flickered between thoughts of past failures and his growing connection with Susan. A strange pull tugged at him, urging him forward.

For someone as straight and unmoving as he, it was a new behavior as he kicked the motorcycle stand to secure it. He'd never investigated a possible criminal act, but this directly affected him. He realized his palm hurt from holding his keys too tightly. When he looked down at his hand, he saw his thumb was on the flashlight attached to the key ring.

For a single moment, he stared, not knowing where to shine the light, his heart pounding in a strange mixture of anticipation and dread, like a dark skeleton whispering mysteries to him. As he walked toward a pile of ashen debris, his boots crunched on the gravel. A shiny object caught his eye, at first making him think the flashlight reflected back, but then realized there was something metallic on the ground, a glint in the snowy white, charred remains.

"What the heck is this?" he whispered to himself as he crouched low to brush the soot and dried branches aside. Beneath the layers of rubble, he uncovered a box, mostly dull from being out in the elements, but as best as he could see in the dim glow of his flashlight not scorched. It must have been buried in the ground where the flames couldn't touch it, and then resurfaced when the snows fell and shifted the earth. It looked oddly out of place amidst the destruction.

Mark's breath hitched as he picked up the heavy tin. His pulse quickened—this was something no one had noticed. His first thought was to tell Susan—not the police. And that very thought made his heart beat in double time.

Mark pulled out his cell and punched in Susan's number. Even now, with the mystery surrounding them, he focused on how soothing her voice was. Like a balm.

"Mark? What's wrong?" she asked, a hint of concern lacing her tone.

"I think I've found something significant."

"What?" He could tell she was trying to keep her

voice calm. So, he would try to calm his, as well, without exposing his increasing excitement, the kind of reaction he'd often felt in the past, but never allowed himself to show anyone else. It wasn't working, he knew she could hear the edge of frenzy in his tone. It would be pretty hard to ignore. Only way to dampen it: just tell her what he'd found. "A tin box was buried under the debris. I'm bringing it over to see what you think."

The long, quiet pause that followed made him wonder if she thought he was a fool, the way Angela would have, but she asked, "Well, are you going to tell me what's inside or do I need to guess?"

He chuckled. "I haven't opened it. I thought we'd do that together."

"Like a Christmas present?" He heard the excitement in her voice. She calmed him in a way no woman had ever, even his Aunt Jenny who'd kept him on track all the way through medical school, tamping down his anxieties, championing his successes. "I'd love…" A voice in the background interrupted Susan. "Mark, it'll have to wait until morning. Ma needs me." The phone went silent before Mark could answer.

A rustle in the far corner of the barn caught his attention. Perspiration dotted his forehead. He lifted the cell and took a video of the entire site. For a brief, surreal moment, he thought he saw a shadow beyond the barn. It seemed to disappear as quickly as it had emerged. He shook his head to rid it of the image. Whoever or whatever it was could be afraid of the video. But in truth, he felt he probably saw nothing. He was brought back into the moment when the rustle of trees began to sway, the bare limbs hitting one another.

Mark felt like a fool in a spooky movie. Shaking his

head and stepping out into the mist, he got back on the motorcycle and rushed away as quickly as he could. "Coward," he thought to himself, then chuckled.

He took one more look behind him at the barn's remains. A wistful vision took hold—as he pictured the out-patient clinic that should have been built there, but for greed. The image dissolved quickly, replaced by the cold reality of what this place had become. A crime scene. A silent witness to deals made in the shadows, where money had likely passed hands for reasons far darker than progress. He could almost see the future in ashes—an out-patient clinic would save so many lives. And maybe, just maybe, it could save his work, too.

Whatever that box contained, it was not just about the clinic. The box, the barn, the study, were all about the future—his and Susan's intertwined.

****

It was close to dawn when Mark rode over to Susan's. He couldn't mistake the excitement on her face as he parked his bike. She stood outside her front door, wrapped tightly in her coat, a knit cap on her head. The wind swept her shiny locks into her face, and she brushed them back.

Mark nodded to Ron sitting across the drive and strode toward Susan, the metal box cool in his hand. As Mark followed her inside, a rush of warmth enveloped him, the rich aroma of freshly brewed coffee that filled his nostrils, all felt like the cozy domesticity he'd always sought. But still, something was off.

The breakfast dishes lingered on the dining room table, untouched and Mrs. Pace sat at the end, her expression weary. Mark hesitated, then moved to a chair nearby, feeling a quiet undercurrent in the air—

something waiting to break.

"Hi, Mrs. Pace," he said, tentatively. The old woman didn't answer, but shifted in her seat. Mark looked at Susan. "I think she's aware I'm here."

"She's in and out." Susan took the box from Mark's hand." She's been listless all night. She senses when I'm tense." Susan put the box on the table. "This thing's an eyesore, I'll give it that," she remarked. They opened it.

Inside: A tangle of paperclips, an old breath mint tin, and a half-filled notebook with Mabel's name on the cover. But beneath the mess—there it was. A single small envelope, unmarked, sealed only with a worn paperclip.

Susan pulled the clip off as she handed it to Mark. She barely contained her excitement as he read the page.

And blinked.

"Holy cow. One hundred thousand dollar Consulting Fee—Paid to: Agricore Development Partners, LLC 'Therapeutic Equipment Purchase— Storage Location: Fuller Barn' Signed: Phillip D. King, MD."

Mark's blood turned to ice. "What? Sue, this could be proof the barn was a laundry for King."

"Agricore is a fake company that Gertie had half-mentioned. The one Harold Fuller had put money in days before the fire.

This wasn't just a receipt. It was a paper trail. A direct link between the stolen clinic funds, the burned-out barn, and Harold's death.

Someone had buried this box in the ground in the barn. Maybe waiting for the right moment. Maybe scared of what it meant.

"Jesus, Susan..." he whispered.

His hand trembled slightly as he slipped the envelope into his coat pocket.

"Dr. Dennis wasn't the chair of the department. He was the man Harold was going to reveal—he was part of this, too."

Mrs. Pace suddenly reached for Susan's hand and let out a shaky breath.

Mrs. Pace lifted her eyes to Mark, and he realized her body moved as she watched him. He sat down next to her.

She groaned.

"You okay, Ma?" she asked as she came back into the dining room and put an arm around her mother.

When Mrs. Pace didn't answer, Mark took the chair beside her.

"I found a receipt in the box. For a hundred thousand dollars. Agricore Development," he said. "Marked for equipment that was supposed to be stored in the Fuller barn."

Her eyes grazed over his.

He pressed on. "I think Harold found out. I think he was going to turn it in."

Still, silence. Then she spoke—her voice like a frayed piece of thread. "He showed it to Gertie, and she showed it to me. The night before the fire. That's why I need to be on the memory machine, honey."

Mark's breath caught.

"You see, Harold told Gertie, and she told me that he'd finally caught Phillip with his hand in the till. Thought he could scare him straight. Said it was just a matter of time before the board turned on him anyway. But Harold..." She gave a faint, broken laugh. "He thought he was invincible. Always did."

Mark's throat tightened. "You think the fire—?"

"—Was set on purpose?" Mrs. Pace turned to him. "Yes."

Susan turned the box upside down, but nothing else fell out. Mark came close to check its interior and their faces practically touched. He caught the soft scent of her shampoo, something clean and floral, and felt her breath brush his cheek as she leaned in. His awareness had shifted—no longer on the charred beams or the collapsed rafters, or this silver box, but on the warmth of her presence beside him. He turned his phone on to show her the video of the interior of the barn.

"Boy, the roof must have collapsed first, because look at that." She pointed to scorched wood consumed by dead branches. Susan took a step forward and Mark grabbed her before she fell into his arms. "Easy there, missy," he laughed. They exchanged a glance, then Susan joined him with a chuckle.

Now they stood shoulder to shoulder, staring down at the puzzle of how Harold Fuller—Gertie's husband—had really died, and where Walter Pace might have escaped to.

"There's more here. Look at this," Susan said quietly, lifting a scorched sheet of paper. The edges curled like dying embers, but the ink was mostly intact. She slid the top page free and held it up between them.

"I believe it's a bank statement. Swiss Private Holdings—Transfer Authorization."

Mark blinked. For a second, the words didn't register. Then he felt Susan's eyes on him, waiting. He gave a short nod. "Keep going."

Her voice tightened. "Clinic accounts. Large withdrawals." She paused. "And here—Dr. King's name."

Mark's stomach clenched.

Susan dug deeper into the singed papers and pulled out another half-burned document. A payroll ledger. Her fingers froze midair.

"My name's on it." Her voice cracked. "Like I've been getting paid…from the very accounts draining Sam Heard Clinic."

Mark's jaw locked. "They were setting you up."

Her face went pale. "Who's been forging payments in my name—making me look complicit?"

The implications fell like a hammer.

Dr. King hadn't just stolen money. He was covering his tracks. And he'd been willing to drag Susan down with him.

Mark swallowed hard, his chest tight. "This isn't just fraud," he said quietly. "It's premeditated murder."

They stood there in silence, the truth settling between them like ash in the air. And in that stillness, Mark felt the shift—not a romantic leap, not yet, but a loyalty. A weight shared. A promise, unspoken.

He didn't reach for her. Didn't need to. They were already in this together.

The room held its breath as Susan scanned the pages. Harold's handwriting was shaky but meticulous—lists of names, coded references to environmental reports, shadowy payments routed through Swiss holdings.

Susan flipped to the next page—and there it was. A bank statement. Dated just weeks before the fire. It showed a large wire transfer from Agricore Holdings to a numbered account connected to the Sam Heard Clinic. And beneath it, in Harold's looping scrawl:

"Shell fund—kickback. Forrester. King. Cover-up."

Mark exhaled slowly. "This isn't just evidence," he said. "It's a roadmap."

"Do we call the news?" Mrs. Pace whispered.

Mark nodded. "And Jamie. He's been waiting for this—anything that could crack it open. Now it's not a cold case. It's prosecutable."

Susan punched in a number on her cell phone. "We have new evidence. Physical proof. Harold Fuller's notebook. Bank records. Names. You need to get to my house right now," Susan told Jaime.

Mark watched her speak with calm, unflinching clarity. When she hung up, everyone looked at her.

"Jaime's on his way," she said. "He's going straight to the District Attorney after he sees this."

Chapter Sixteen

"Mabel's dead," Mrs. Pace repeated as she stared at Susan for support. "Honey, I don't know how much time I have to be…awake. Please. I knew Gertie and her husband. I loved them both and Harold didn't deserve to die like that. And now Mabel. I need to be on Mark's machine."

"Ma, I'm scared. I don't know what the enzyme would do to you and your diagnosis is…"

"Getting worse," Her mother threw her napkin on the table. "I already know that. And I know you need to give consent, Susan. But there are memories of Walter that I can't get to, and I want to remember. He was a great father, a terrible husband. But we both loved you girls. You and…and…"

"Pamela. My sister's name is Pamela."

"Susan," her mother's voice even more urgent. "I know things that might stop the clinic from closing."

Susan stared at Mark. "She would know things, Mark. But this is my mother. Please. Don't let anything bad happen here."

"I don't want to chance it, Mrs. Pace."

Mrs. Pace's stare began to wane. Mark instinctively reached for Susan's hand, squeezing it gently. She appeared visibly shaken.

Susan turned to Mark. "I'll sign if you're willing to take a chance. Don't shut anything down. We still might be able to save the clinic and reveal criminal activity if my mother remembers things."

The front door swung open and Pamela, brushing off her coat and pulling off a knit cap, stepped inside. Snow fell on the foyer as she hung the coat on the rack, then stopped. "I just heard the last part of that. Ma? Oh hi, Mark." Pam extended her hand toward Mark as she balanced Zoe on her knee.

"Tell them, Pammie. I need to tell what I know, and I can't remember it." Her mother called into the front hallway.

Pamela moved into the dining room slowly. "You want to put her on the machine? For what purpose." Pamela checked her watch. "My shift starts at eleven. When do you want to do this?"

"Right now," her mother answered Pam. "Mabel's dead." The old woman held her heart as she shook her head. "My moments of reality seem to be coming in closer proximity to each other. I probably sound like the high school English teacher I once was." Ma wavered and then fell forward.

"Mom!" Susan leapt from her seat, catching her mother just before she could fall to the floor. Mark was already at her side, his doctor's instincts kicking in with laser focus.

"Clear the table," he ordered, his voice firm but steady. Pamela rushed to move dishes as Susan and Mark gently laid her mother on the tablecloth. Her breathing was shallow, her skin pale.

"She's unresponsive," Mark murmured, pressing two fingers to her neck. "Her pulse is weak. We need to get her to the clinic—now."

Susan's heart pounded as she helped lift her mother

S. A. Stolin

into Mark's arms. Pamela grabbed Zoe and the car keys, and together they rushed into the snowy night, the glow of Christmas decorations blurring as they sped toward Sam Heard Clinic. Pamela called Brad and when he arrived, she handed Zoe off to him. "I'm staying here with my mother," she said.

Beverly was already waiting at the entrance, alerted by Mark's urgent call. The staff hurried into action as they wheeled her mom into the examination room. Mark worked swiftly, his hands steady as he examined her vitals.

"We need to stabilize her," he said, his mind racing. Susan put a mask over her mother's nose and the oxygen flowed as they monitored the stats. In a few moments, her mother sprang upright.

"I couldn't breathe for a moment," she said. "I remembered last Christmas and Harold dying in that fire. And I had images." She grabbed Susan's arm. "Images of the man who came running out the back when we all ran to see what was on fire. Sue, I saw him, but I can't remember his name. I know who it was. I need to get on Mark's machine. Please. You see, honey, the man who was the 'ghost' wasn't a ghost at all, he was a very old man. One I'd never laid eyes on before."

****

Hospitals had a different glow at night—almost sacred, like whispered prayers. The soft gleam of overhead lights reflected off polished floors, casting long shadows, the sterile scent of antiseptic mixing with the faint aroma of coffee from the nurses' station.

Mark stepped through the double doors of the auditorium, his pulse steady, but his mind on high alert. Beside him, Susan moved with quiet determination,

162

Pamela and Mrs. Pace trailing just behind. The moment they entered, he took control.

Without hesitation, he vaulted onto the platform. The machine stood at the center, waiting. Untouched. Or was it?

His chest tightened as he approached it, fingers grazing its surface. Every nerve in his body screamed for him to be cautious. He knew too well how easily things could be sabotaged.

Stay calm. Check everything.

He ran his hands over the panel, his trained eyes scanning for the slightest disturbance. A disconnected wire, a misplaced screw—any proof that someone had tampered with his life's work. But everything was as it should be. For now.

Mark exhaled slowly, shoving down his paranoia, and turned back to the others, his gaze locking onto Susan's. Concern flickered in her expression, but beneath it—trust. He would see this through. No matter what it cost him.

Susan wheeled her mother to the front of the monitor, and watched as Mark sprayed her arm with the anesthetic and then placed the IV in a vein. He turned on the monitor and its bright screen illuminated the room, the familiar soft hum began to vibrate. Susan turned her phone to a station where a gentle melody played in the background, one of Mrs. Pace's favorite songs from her youth, Susan whispered to him.

The lights in the auditorium had been dimmed to a warm hush. Mrs. Pace sat reclined in the memory chair, her shoulders fragile against the stark white linen, the lines of age on her face like softened etchings from another life.

Susan sat close beside her, her hand steady, her voice low and coaxing. Mark stood behind them, silent but alert. He was surprised it felt like they had always worked together—two minds with one purpose, hearts beating in quiet tandem. This was what they did best. Together.

"Mom," Susan whispered gently, "We're going to take you on a little journey back in time today."

The room was silent, except for the rhythmic breathing of Mrs. Pace. Minutes ticked by each one stretching longer than the last, and then—a change.

Mrs. Pace's eyes fluttered slightly as the fog of dementia that had clouded her gaze for so long seemed to lift, as if the music stirred something deep within her.

As the machine pulsated, Susan's photographs appeared on the monitor's screen. Their worn edges weren't visible in the display, but they were treasures—moments frozen in time. "Do you remember these, Mom?" Susan asked, her voice soft and coaxing.

Mark hit the button, and a photograph appeared of golden balloons which hung from the ceiling of a grand ballroom.

Susan's breath caught as she pointed. "That's you and Dad, on your wedding day."

Mrs. Pace's gaze lingered on the image, her hand lifting—trembling, hesitant—until her fingertips pointed to the screen. A flicker of recognition crossed her face, fragile yet unmistakable.

Mark adjusted the enzyme flow, carefully increasing the dosage. For a brief moment, the blank stare of a woman lost to time shifted. Her lips parted slightly, as if words were forming, memories hovering just out of reach.

Susan leaned in. "Mom?"

The machine hummed softly. The next image appeared.

"I-I remember," Mrs. Pace whispered.

Susan leaned closer, her eyes brimming with hope. "Mom, do you remember the fire?"

Mrs. Pace's lips parted. "Phillip King." The name was more breath than voice, but it echoed like a gavel in the quiet space.

Susan leaned in slightly, watching as a trace of color bloomed on the older woman's cheeks. Her face relaxing—her memory unspooling.

"It was Gertie's husband, Harold."

"Where was my father in all this? Where was Walter Pace?"

Her mother looked up at Susan. "He disappeared after he'd made a small investment in an outpatient clinic that Phillip and Harold had touted as a great investment in research. Ha! Phillip told them he wanted to support the town. But Walter told me what Harold found instead…was siphoned funds, redirected accounts, money disappearing into shadows. Not for condos. Not for a flashy development.

"What I couldn't remember was your father said an old man grabbed Harold as the flames erupted—" Mrs. Pace dropped her head and cried. "—He kept yelling at him: 'No, no, Harold. Don't let King trick you like this. I'll handle it, I'll handle it.' "

"Who? Who would handle it?" Mark came out from behind the machine.

"The ghost. He was the silent partner—the man Walter said Harold trusted. He told Harold about Eric Forrester. Phillip King's nephew. A young man with failing kidneys and no time left. A transplant was his only chance. And the funds? Misappropriated, by King as each check came in—signed by King, but repurposed, and hidden behind a fire that would erase all proof. And killing Harold—" Mrs. Pace grabbed her head and shook it back and forth, tears streaming down her face. "The Ghost grabbed Harold, and he must have thought he'd saved him, but he disappeared. All that fire, all that heat, everyone running. And Harold—bless him—he'd threatened to expose it all."

"And he paid for that threat with his life." Susan shook her head. She swallowed hard. "So much loss. So much silence. And yet here it is, finally, in the open."

Mark stood silently waiting for more, then as if a weight the size of a boulder had been lifted, Mrs. Pace let out a breath she must've been holding for years.

Her lips barely moved, but her voice held the weight of a woman unburdening her soul. "I didn't want to believe it. But I knew. I knew, I knew he'd chosen to put a stop to the theft. I wanted Walter to come forward, but he left. No note, no word at all."

Susan reached for her hand, a soft squeeze of reassurance. "You've helped us more than you know, Ma," she said gently.

Mrs. Pace gave the faintest smile, a peace settling in her eyes. "Please take me home. I need to sleep."

Mark shut down the machine and moved into the light, taking Susan's hand.

The room was still. But the truth had finally moved.

And everything—everything—was about to change.

"We have more to take to Jaime McPherson. This case will be air tight against King, but what about Eric Forrester? Mark paced across the stage. His thoughts spinning. Pausing, he slowly said, "Susan, do you think Eric's The Ghost?"

"Susan, Susan," Mrs. Pace gurgled. "I still feel confused, but it's less than ever." She looked over her shoulder at her daughter, the bond between them, to Mark, seemed to be stronger than ever.

He thumbed Susan's tears off her cheeks, and she gazed into his eyes. "You gave me my mother back longer than she's been for months."

They stood in silence for a moment, the weight of their success settling over them. "Think of all the lives we can change now, all the hope we can restore."

Mrs. Pace studied her hands. The light in her eyes no longer bright.

Susan apparently saw it, too, but it looked to Mark like she realized, they had gotten her mother to the present and kept her there longer than they'd anticipated. This wasn't just a victory for science; it was a victory for love, for connection, and for family.

****

Once they returned to Susan's house, and put Mrs. Pace in her bed, they sat at the kitchenette table and drank tea.

"I can't believe I didn't go out to the barn sooner," Susan said. "Why didn't I at least find out what everyone was talking about when it burned down. I figured it was just a fire hazard. Now I'm sorry I didn't."

"You're a doctor, not a detective," Mark said.

"You probably didn't want to know Daddy's involvement," Pamela offered.

But Mark shook his head. "Gertie's memory of that night seemed vivid, but flawed. Maybe the trauma is still too horrible for her to remember clearly."

"Mark, we'll keep talking to her. Possibly in time, she can corroborate the facts."

"I don't mean to sound completely paranoid, but Susan, I saw a shadow out there, too."

"And in that box there was a note written in someone's hand that looks like it was meant to go to the FBI but was never sent."

"Maybe Jaime can figure out more of this mess." Susan yawned. "Well, once again, I'm calling it a night," Mark leaned over and kissed her mouth. The kiss lingered, long and deep. Susan didn't push away, and pulled him to her, her arms tight around his body. She slid out of his embrace and stared into his eyes, full of something—love, caring? She couldn't be sure. Maybe just a "thank you."

Their faces were only inches apart. "Susan…"

"I know," she said.

Mark nodded, the warmth of the moment still lingering, though unspoken as he walked the front door. "Oh, well, a nice jaunt down the hill to my cabin will be revitalizing. See you tomorrow." One last kiss and he was gone.

Chapter Seventeen

"I'm calling a board meeting," Mark told Beverly once he got back in the clinic the next day. No one was running the Unit now. With King under arrest, and his nephew, who knew where? No one was at the clinic except Mark.

"Mrs. Fogelson, this is Mark Moore, oh, you do know who I am," he said as he dialed the first name on the board's list. "Well, thank you, ma'am. I need to call an emergency board meeting. I'm wondering if you can round up the rest of the members and let's meet in the recreation room this afternoon?" He listened a moment to the old woman's frantic answer.

"Yes, ma'am. We need a new Chairman of the Department. I'm sure you heard the rumors. They're true. Dr. King was arrested."

Mark hung up, and slumped into his worn leather chair. Frustration burned in his chest as he slammed the draft of his results of the three patients who'd been on his machine, onto his desk. That was it. Three was not a big enough number to get real data. Not enough to prove anything.

Leaning back, he tented his hands under his chin. Would his work ever be taken seriously? The study was still in its infancy, the numbers too small. He needed more cases—more proof. But how long would the board give him before pulling the plug?

As he contemplated his fate, wondering how he would save the Unit, Eric Forrester appeared in his doorframe. Mark stood.

"I called Harvard. They have no record of you."

Forrester's face turned white. "You had no right—"

"I have every right. You've been undermining me and Susan from day one. You've been hiding a secret for too long, Eric."

"I need help. I don't have a long time and I'm fading. Will you help me?"

"Your uncle burned down a barn that was to be turned into an outpatient clinic and killed people. You're complicit."

"I'm not. I never…" Eric moved into Mark's office.

Mark clenched his hands into fists to keep from slugging the man.

"I…" Eric glanced over his shoulder as if to make sure they were alone. "I found"—his voice barely above a whisper—"documents my uncle tried to destroy in the fire." Eric's face paled with each word he uttered.

Mark took in his body. He was more feeble than before.

"I need you to call some place that would take me in an experimental situation."

Mark looked at the young man. He was thinner than before, his eyes red and blurred. His speech low. He was barely able to stand on his own. While he had benefitted from stolen money, if what he'd revealed was true, then he wasn't all bad.

"Did you get Mr. Fuller out of the barn?"

"No." He shook his head. "I saw my uncle running into the woods calling Mr. Fuller's name."

"So you knew your uncle killed Harold."

Eric's head dropped to his chest. "I suspected after I came back from my first treatment. I waited until my aunt and uncle were out of town, and took the box with the evidence to the barn and shoved it beneath some boards."

"Does Detective McPherson know?"

"Yes," he sighed. "I told him everything. He's weighing the option to charge me, too, but considering my illness, he doubts I'll live long enough to go to trial."

Mark nodded and picked up the receiver on his desk phone and dialed. "I need to put a patient under the care of the nephrologist—he needs a transplant, but perhaps you can assist him until a kidney becomes available."

When he hung up the phone, Mark handed Eric a piece of paper. "They'll see you. No one gets turned away." As Eric reached for it, Mark grabbed his hand. "You'll be arrested afterward, I can promise you that."

"Better than being dead," he said, and pulled the paper away.

Mark watched as Forrester stumbled out of the office and closed the door behind him.

****

The board meeting took place at exactly three p.m. as Mrs. Fogelson hobbled into the recreation room, followed by the only other woman on the board, Elsie Butterworth, a middle-aged woman with tight gray curls and oversized red glasses.

Mr. Johnson moved into the room and stood beside Mark, who was at the end of a long table that had five chairs for the board members. Bert Mandel, a highly respected cardiologist sat next to Mrs. Fogelson and Mr. Horton and Mr. Wayland, two elderly gentlemen with hearing aids and canes sat on the end.

Mr. Johnson raised his voice before the meeting was called to order. "You, dear friends, are about to witness first hand, this man's extraordinary genius."

"I wouldn't go that far," Mark managed to blurt out.

"Lord knows how long this clinic will be solvent and now you have proof Dr. Moore's machine is viable."

The members nodded.

Mrs. Fogelson adjusted her glasses and said, "Dr. Moore, I'm willing to put everything on the line for this machine, but too much money has been—lost. No one can find the money we've allocated. It simply disappeared and other projects have suffered. If your machine delivers, it will elevate Sam Heard Clinic to global recognition and funds will no longer be a problem."

Board members nodded in agreement. Mark heard their murmurs of approval. But none of it was going to matter if Susan wasn't on board. If she suspected he was keeping her out of their study, cheating her the way Dr. Dennis had, all was lost anyway. His focus was brought back by John Horton.

He adjusted his rimless glasses and pursed his lips, as he sat prim and erect in the front row next to Mrs. Fogelson. "I'm heart-sick that Mabel is gone. I loved her. I knew her for years. So, Dr. Moore, who will you demonstrate on now? There's fear surrounding this machine. When and where is your formal study going to be submitted?"

"I have the figures on three people. If you will let me have two more, including Mr. Johnson, here, I think you will be pleasantly surprised how the machine will expose cognitive decline sooner than folks want to face it."

"And I am personally volunteering to be on this machine," Mr. Johnson announced. "You see, I know there are more hidden truths that need to be uncovered."

"I thought all that was just settled, for Heaven's sake," Bert Mandel yelled.

Dr. Mandel, who wore thick rimmed glasses added, "Remember, nothing from these experiments can be introduced in court."

"Whether or not it's introduced and accepted doesn't really matter if the judge allows proof of positive demonstrations," Mark said. He turned to Mr. Johnson. "Are you comfortable to be on the machine?"

"Of course, I am. That's why I'm running up and down these halls, trying to keep up with you, Doctor, and I must say it isn't always easy." He turned an accusatory glance at the board members. "I don't need to be asked a hundred times if I want to be on the machine. My lover, Mabel Le Triel, is gone. Dead."

A shocked silence followed. Mark thought he'd intrinsically known that the two were together, but hadn't really thought a lot about it.

"And let me tell you something," Mr. Johnson said. "If she had faith in it, well, by golly, so do I." Mr. Johnson offered a tight smile of enthusiasm. He looked around the table at the five board members. "No siree, I'm not letting a few dirty dogs close this clinic."

Mark's lips twitched into a small smile. "Okay, let's do it." He could only hope for a positive outcome.

Bert stood and pulled his chair from behind the desk and stood next to Rodney who'd just arrived.

"There you are, sir," Rodney said to Mr. Johnson who sat heavily in the wheelchair Rodney had wheeled into the room. After squirming in the seat a few seconds, he rubbed his hands. "The incompetence in this place is legion."

"Dr. Moore I think you might consider putting him on the machine right now. If I might be so bold. When he's enthusiastic like this, he's at his best." Rodney immediately helped Mr. Johnson back in his wheelchair, looking embarrassed for the old man's outburst.

"Please follow me again, ladies and gentlemen, into the auditorium."

****

Mark adjusted the settings on the memory machine, his fingers hovering over the controls. Something didn't sit right. He hesitated, glancing over at Mr. Johnson sitting comfortably, Rodney behind him.

The old man grinned, but there was a sharpness behind his eyes—too sharp for someone with cognitive decline.

Mark's gut twisted. He held the IV and the freeze canister, but he couldn't move. This wasn't right. His hands moved before his brain even finished his thought. He put the IV tubing back into the drawer with the cannister and switched off the machine. The soft hum died instantly.

"No," Mark said firmly. "You're not going on my machine."

Board members gasped.

"I'm not traipsing somewhere else," Mrs. Fogelson announced. "My arthritis is killing me. You got a machine for that, too, doctor?"

Mr. Johnson chuckled. "Don't worry, this boy right here's a smart man. If he doesn't have a machine for that yet, he'll devise one, I guarantee it." Mr. Johnson leaned forward in his wheelchair, a flicker of satisfaction crossing his face. He studied the faces of the board members. One at a time. "I want all of you to know—my dementia was always a ruse," he said. "Yep, that's right. An act. I needed to find out what happened to the barn, and to protect Mabel. I loved her and I was concerned about her safety here, that's why I checked myself into the clinic. But mainly I wanted to see what kind of underhanded things were happening. Things that could destroy the work being done for dementia patients. I didn't want to lose my love." His voice cracked, and he wiped away a tear. "But old age…"

The board members stiffened as Mr. Johnson's gaze swept over them. He stared them down, his presence suddenly towering despite the wheelchair.

"I was the 'ghost'. That damn barn…it sat on land with significant environmental contamination. Old pesticides, heavy metals in the soil. Agricore wouldn't touch it unless it was clear. Dennis was the first to suggest we torch it. Harold, Walter Pace, and I disagreed." He rubbed his face. "Harold was the only one who knew I was the silent partner. Harold told me he was confronting Dennis and King. He didn't care that Agricore would pay well for the land once the barn was burned down. When I arrived the barn was already on fire, and Harold was pushing his way through the flames. I grabbed him and we hightailed it through the woods. I thought he was right behind me, but he must have gone back. Later, I learned his death was ruled an accident. I wanted to go to the police, but by that time Walter had disappeared, and it would be my word against theirs."

There was a shift in the auditorium. The atmosphere thickened.

I told Mabel all about it. See Walter and I were

drinking buddies, but no one could hold their liquor compared to him and he babbled and babbled about everything when he was high. I told my love, I told Mabel, to document everything, and now you have her dying declaration and I think it will go far in court."

Mark sighed, his thoughts floating to Mabel Le Triel. His heart swelled with an understanding that Mr. Johnson was standing up for his love.

Everyone seemed to glare at everyone else and Mark realized it was his turn to do some encouraging. He swallowed his fury and asked gently, "Think of the difference that money would have really made for this place."

Mr. Johnson laid his head against the back rest of the wheelchair. "A lot of difference." He raised his head and pointed to the door. "Get my daughter in here, will ya, sonny?"

Elizabeth stood quietly by the doors. She was tall, slender, beautifully dressed and her short hair perfectly coiffed. She came forward, but before she could step up to the stage, Mr. Johnson called down to her.

"Honey, I want you to get Switzerland on the phone. I want money transferred to this clinic right now. I'm personally gonna fund it—make sure it's financed."

A murmur followed, and Mrs. Fogelson stood. "Thank you, Ezra. I gotta be honest with you, we all thought you were getting to be a crazy old coot. But you're a very fine man."

The other members of the board clapped.

"Not on your life, honey bunny," he answered, a ripple of laughter in his voice. "Get some for this Forrester kid, too. Money's everywhere, folks. There's a ton of it out there. No reason for it to sit when people need it."

"And I think it's time for you all to designate a new Chief of Alzheimer's," Mark said. "And I think it should be Dr. Susan Pace, if she agrees."

The board members clapped harder in unison.

"Hear, hear," Dr. Mandel said. "I agree, but where is Susan?"

****

With the meeting concluded, Mark tore down the hall, his pulse hammering. A surge of excitement mingled with hope, tightening in his chest as he reached the reception desk.

"Hold it," Bev called out. "She's not at home. She saw the study on your desk. You didn't include her in the author's section." Mark stopped short. "Mark, she swore me to secrecy, but that's exactly what happened with Herman Dennis. He published without her, humiliating her. Now she thinks you've done the same thing."

"Why didn't she say anything? I would have told her this is only a draft. I wanted to present a draft to King, to show him we were making progress, but with everything that's happened, I didn't have time to change it."

Beverly lowered her head, then hovered over a piece of paper. She wrote something and scooted it across the desk to Mark. "Don't say it was from me. She loves the Cove at Carmel. She's angry, Mark. She thought she could trust you."

"She can. I'll make it up to her." He grabbed the piece of paper and kissed Beverly's hand. "Thanks, Bev."

"Good luck, and Merry Christmas—in two days. I hope you bought her a present." Beverly remained leaning over the counter, a wide grin on her face, as Mark pushed out the doors.

Chapter Eighteen

The drive to Carmel was a blur of winding roads and pounding thoughts. Mark replayed every conversation he and Susan ever had, every moment he'd spent working on the paper with her always in mind. He should have double-checked, should have made sure her name was included even if it was just a draft. How could he have been so careless?

When he finally arrived to the beach town, it wasn't hard to find the address Beverly had given him. Little houses dotted boardwalk that led to the sand. He parked in front of the main entrance, and sat back for a moment to take in the setting sun which cast a golden glow over the waves. He spotted her through the living room window, curled up on the couch.

He jumped up the two plank stairs to her door, but she opened it before he could knock, her expression guarded.

"Mark," she said, her voice cool. "Why are you here?"

"Susan, please let me explain," he began, stepping toward her.

She put out a hand and stopped him.

He shook his head. "The draft—I made a mistake. I was going to include your name on the final version. You know how much I've come to value you, your work. I—" He ran a hand through his hair, his voice breaking. "—

I'm so sorry. I never meant to hurt you."

Susan looked unfazed and for a moment, he thought she might simply ask him to leave. But she exhaled and nodded toward the living room.

"Come in."

"You know what it's like to be humiliated? Shunned," she said. "Well, that's how I felt. I gave Dr. Dennis…"

"Too much." He finished her sentence for her. "But you were showing off for him. You wanted to impress him."

"You're smart." she smiled. "I did, but that didn't mean my talk therapy wasn't working. It didn't mean I didn't know what I was doing. He stole my values and planned on working with you, leaving me out entirely." Tears formed in her eyes. "That's how he planned on breaking up with me, too. He didn't have the guts to just call it off. He wanted to make me so miserable, I'd do it for him and then leave."

"I would never do that to you. And you know it. Look what we've been through together," he said.

Suddenly, she leaned forward and kissed him. "I do know. But it brought back terrible memories. And you left it sitting right on your desk, Mark. Did you hope I'd see it?"

"Of course not. It was a mistake, my love, honestly. The final study will have our names together. Why didn't you ask me?"

"I still don't trust," she cried and buried her head in his chest, then looked up into his eyes. "I love you Mark. Is it safe to love you?"

"Sue, come on. I'm putting your name on every single draft after this one, scout's honor." He raised his hand with three fingers showing the Boy Scout pledge. "And I won't submit anything until you've seen it."

She smiled, but he could sense she was still a little put off. "Okay."

****

Mark barely remembered ordering dinner, but at some point, Chinese takeout had arrived. Now, half-empty containers littered the coffee table, the scent of soy and ginger lingering in the air. He and Susan had eaten in companionable silence, the weight of the day pressing down on them—an unseen force. The flickering lamplight cast soft shadows across her face, and for the first time in hours, the tension between them wasn't laced with fear—but something deeper, unspoken.

After putting away the remnants of the meal, they first sat on the couch, separated by the pillow Susan had put between them, her arm casually lying across it.

"So, did the board meeting happen?"

He nodded.

"Okay. What happened?" she asked, staring straight ahead, out a latticed window.

Mark leaned across the pillow, threw it to the floor and in one swift motion, he pulled her to him, his mouth capturing hers in a long kiss. He drew back, his gaze burned into hers.

"The last thing I'm thinking about right now is the board meeting. It was successful, shall we say?"

And Susan snuggled into his arms.

"Because the coup de grâce is, the board has elected *you* to be the new Chief of the Alzheimer's Unit."

Chow mein almost flew out of her mouth. "No. You should be."

"No, ma'am. It's your time. Congratulations."

Later that night, as they lay tangled together, Mark felt her warmth pressed against him, the steady crash of the ocean the only sound. For the first time in weeks, a sense of peace settled over him.

In the early morning, he stretched before he opened his eyes, and when he stirred, turning to reach across the bed for Susan, his hand met only cool sheets. His eyes blinked open, adjusting to the dim light filtering through the curtains.

Susan was gone.

He pushed himself up, listening. Slipping out of bed, he padded to the doorway and leaned against the frame. There she was, out on the beach, barefoot in the sand, her robe pulled tightly around her as she cradled a steaming mug. He watched her from the door as she stared at the horizon, motionless but obviously deep in thought. The waves rolled in steady and slow, giving off a serene picture, but Mark knew better.

He knew what was on her mind. That same distrust that had pulled him out of bed at different times before dawn.

For a moment, he just watched her, taking in the way the wind tugged at her hair, the way she sat on the beach—strong, yet vulnerable. Then, quietly, he stepped forward, his bare feet sinking into the cool sand.

Mark shuffled toward her, his hair tousled from sleep, a blanket wrapped around his shoulders. Susan turned, as he reached her and sat, slipping his arm around her shoulder.

"Couldn't sleep, huh?" he asked softly.

She shook her head. "Just thinking."

He drew her face to his. "About what?"

"I'm still scared, Mark. Now I've got the unit on my

hands, too. What I wanted badly is freaking me out. I'm waiting for the other shoe to drop, and I can't go through that again."

He cupped her face in his hands, his eyes steady on hers. "I'm not Herman Dennis. I'm not anyone else. I'm me, Susan. And I love you."

He couldn't believe he'd just said that. Was he really ready to admit that?

****

Susan stared at him, open, no judgment. She could feel her heart skip a beat. *Don't ruin this,* she told herself, pressing her eyes shut as she sipped the coffee. *Don't overthink it.* But the voice in her head was relentless. *He'll believe I only want his research. He won't trust me any more than I trusted him. It's what she deserved.*

She let out a shaky breath and jumped to her feet, but he reached and pulled her back down.

"No, don't go."

Susan sat back on her haunches.

There was a strange look in his eyes. He adjusted his body so that he knelt in the sand and reached into his robe's pocket.

Susan took in a deep breath and put her hands to her face. He trusts me. She was wrong, he did believe in her.

He pulled out a small velvet box.

She jumped to her feet, her head shaking back and forth in disbelief.

Mark stared at her, and her heart was overwhelmed.

"This was my mother's," he said. "I never really knew her. Aunt Jenny brought me up after the…accident. And told me to give this to the person who is my soul-mate."

Susan reached out and covered his mouth with a

finger.

He kissed it, then added, "Susan," his voice thick with emotion, "will you marry me? Let's face whatever comes next together."

Tears spilled down her cheeks, and she nodded, as he pulled himself to his feet. "Yes," she whispered. "Yes."

He lifted off the sand and kissed her, and slipped the beautiful diamond ring onto her finger, as he pulled her into a kiss.

The waves crashed behind them, as the sun rose on a new chapter of their lives. And Susan knew she could finally trust a man.

"You wanted to make sure I knew I could trust you. Oh, Mark, I love you."

"We need to get to the clinic early tomorrow morning."

"Why?"

"I think you'll understand the minute we get there."

****

The auditorium at Sam Heard International Clinic was packed—doctors, nurses, researchers, and staff filling every seat. A hush fell over the room as Mark Moore stepped onto the stage, the bright overhead lights casting a stark glow over his face. He wasn't a man who enjoyed public speaking, but this moment was too important.

At the podium, he cleared his throat, his gaze scanning the audience until he found her.

Susan.

Seated in the front row, she looked poised but slightly apprehensive, her hands folded neatly in her lap. Only he noticed the way her fingers fidgeted slightly, the pink flush creeping up her neck.

Mark took a breath. This was long overdue.

"I want to thank you all for gathering here today," he began, his voice steady but filled with emotion. "As many of you know, our research into Alzheimer's and memory retrieval has taken some unexpected turns—some breakthroughs, some setbacks, and more than a little controversy. But through it all, one thing has remained clear."

He glanced at Susan again, and this time, he let his voice soften just a little.

"We wouldn't be standing here today without Dr. Susan Pace."

A murmur of surprise rippled through the room. Susan sat straighter, eyes widening, her blush deepening.

Mark continued.

"She wasn't just instrumental in this study. She is the study. The memory machine wouldn't be what it is today if not for Susan—her work, her insight, and her courage to be one half of this clinical trial. She put herself on the line for this research. And because of her, we've made discoveries that could change the way we approach memory retrieval forever."

As Mark waited for the thundering applause to die down. He looked at Susan. She ducked her head slightly. A flicker of pride filled him.

"But beyond that," he added, his voice growing more personal, "she's the heart of this place. Many of you have worked alongside her—you know dedication, her ability to fight for patients when the rest of us are stuck in the data. I want you all to know that going forward, Dr. Susan Pace is the one leading our Alzheimer's research. She will be at the helm of this unit, and with her at the forefront, I have no doubt that Sam Heard will become the global leader in dementia care and research."

The applause swelled again, louder this time.

Susan's lips parted in shock, her eyes locking onto his.

Mark stepped away from the podium, walking toward her as people turned in their seats to look at her, to see her as the leader she'd become. He held out a hand. "Dr. Pace?"

A soft, almost breathless laugh escaped her lips. Then she rose.

****

The staff rose first. Then the nurses. Then the entire auditorium followed, rising to their feet like a wave cresting toward the woman at center stage. Mark saw Beverly in the front row, her hand high in the air, waving like a proud sister.

Applause thundered around them, echoing off the high ceilings like a storm of gratitude. Mark's chest tightened. Susan stood frozen for a heartbeat, her lips parted in disbelief. The spotlight caught the shimmer in her eyes.

She wasn't just being recognized.

She was being seen. *Truly* seen—for the woman she was. For the heart she gave to this place, to these people.

And Mark had been a part of that. Of course, she'd done it for herself, but he'd been there for her completely. *For her.*

Not for the study. Not for the hospital. Not even for himself.

For her.

Their eyes locked across the distance. In that instant,

everything else fell away. He gave her a quiet, deliberate smile—one that told her she didn't have to say a word.

Because he already knew.

And God help him, he would move heaven and earth to keep seeing her like this—for the rest of his life.

****

Later that evening, on the porch where they had first argued and solidified a bond that neither thought was possible, Mark stood at the railing and watched the city lights twinkling below. He was waiting, waiting for her.

He heard her before he saw her. The soft click of her heels as she came out of the entrance to the clinic. He watched the way she exhaled, slowly, before stepping up beside him.

"You didn't have to do that," Susan said, her voice gentle.

"Yes, I did."

She shook her head, letting out a half-laugh, half-sigh. "You blindsided me."

"Good," he said simply. "It's about time everyone sees you the way I do." Her expression softened. "Mark…"

Before she could find the words, he reached for her hands. Warm. Strong. Steady.

"I meant what I said back there," he murmured. "About us. About what we're building. I don't just want to work with you, Susan. I want a life with you. A family. A future."

She stared at him, something unreadable flickering behind her eyes. Then, slowly, she whispered, "That's what I want, too."

A small smile pulled at his lips. "Good."

She chuckled, shaking her head again, but this time,

her fingers laced through his. "We make a great team."

Mark's gaze darkened with emotion. "Yeah, we do."

The silence stretched, but it wasn't uncomfortable. It was full. Full of everything unsaid. Everything promised.

Then, finally, Susan leaned in, closing the last of the space between them.

Their lips met—a slow, deep kiss. It wasn't just passion. It was commitment.

A beginning.

A future.

Chapter Nineteen

As Mark stepped into the Pace house, warmth wrapped around him. The scent of cinnamon and pine filled his lungs, mingling with the faint crackle of the fire in the stone hearth. Twinkling lights framed the windows, their glow reflecting off the fresh snowfall outside.

His gaze swept over the dining room. Susan had outdone herself. The table was set with fine china, crystal glasses, and an elegant centerpiece of holly and red candles. Everything perfect, carefully arranged.

A Christmas Eve dinner straight out of a postcard.

Pamela bustled around the kitchen, balancing a tray of roasted vegetables while her year-old daughter, Zoe, giggled in her high chair, her tiny hands smearing mashed potatoes across the tray. Mark smiled at the scene, feeling a rare sense of home he hadn't known in years.

Susan, seated beside him, nudged his elbow. "You keep staring like you've never seen a toddler make a mess before."

He chuckled. "Not like this. Zoe is an artist."

Pamela laughed from the kitchen doorway. "An artist of destruction."

Mrs. Pace, seated at the head of the table, remained quiet through most of dinner, eating slowly, her movements deliberate. She had been having good days and bad days, and tonight seemed to fall somewhere in between. Susan and Pamela kept a close watch, exchanging silent glances of concern.

Brad walked in still dressed in his brown hospital uniform.

"Sorry folks. A hospital never stops."

He sat down between Pamela and Susan. He leaned into Pamela and gave her a kiss. Halfway through dessert, Mark rose, a glass of champagne in his hand. "I propose a toast to the next Chief of the service, Dr. Susan Pace. And the first female leader of the service, I might add. As well as my future wife."

Mrs. Pace raised her glass. "Thank you to my beautiful children."

Mark kissed Susan and as they finished a perfect Christmas Eve dinner.

Zoe asked, "Do I get a puppy?"

Epilogue

Another year had finally come to Crescent Hill and to Sam Heard Clinic. The freezing cold winter had given way to a crisp, sunny morning and the garden in front of the Clinic was in full bloom, bustling with life as patients and staff mingled for the clinic's next annual Alzheimer's Awareness fundraiser. Bright banners fluttered in the breeze, and a small stage had been set up again, this time under a canopy of trees. The scent of fresh flowers mixed with the salty air drifting in from the lake below, and Zoe, playing with her year old furry pup, created an atmosphere of renewal.

Susan stood at the edge of the crowd, watching the joyful energy that seemed to ripple through the gathering. It was more than just a fundraiser—it was a celebration of life, of memories reclaimed and futures restored. Her shiny engagement ring sparkled in the light, but her eyes drifted to the stage where Mark was tuning his guitar, preparing to play a few songs for the crowd since it had been such a pleasure before. His two colleagues from the last Alzheimer's Christmas Festival, Clem, and Stan. They bowed to Susan as Mark caught her gaze and winked, the look in his eyes so different from the guarded man who had arrived last year.

Beside Susan, Gertie Fuller sat quietly in her wheelchair. A huge balloon with the bright pink number "71" wafting in the breeze. She gazed out at the garden.

Despite the laughter and festive air, there was a subtle melancholy in her expression. She reached for Susan's hand, squeezing it gently.

"I wish Mabel were here to see this," Gertie said softly.

Susan nodded, her heart tightening at the mention of their dear friend Mabel Le Triel. Her absence was still felt deeply by everyone who had been at the clinic when Mark first arrived.

"She would've loved this," Susan replied. She had been relieved when the coroner's report had declared Mabel had died in her sleep. "The music, the crowd…it would've been her moment to shine."

Gertie chuckled softly, though her voice was tinged with sadness. "Yes, she always loved being the center of attention. But more than that, she loved dancing and sharing her stories. I can still see her lifting that right leg onto the mattress and stretching." Gertie's voice cracked. "I can hear her, clear as day, telling tales of Broadway and romance."

Susan's eyes misted as she recalled Mabel's infectious energy. "She had a way of lighting up every room she entered. Even now, I half-expect her to come sweeping in, dressed to the nines, ready to steal the show."

Gertie smiled, her eyes glistening. "She would've made quite an entrance, wouldn't she?"

Susan nodded. "She always did." They sat in a comfortable silence for a moment, both of them lost in memories of Mabel. The garden around them buzzed with activity, but for a few moments, it felt as though time had slowed, allowing them to honor their friend's memory in the midst of the celebration.

The music began as Mark strummed the opening chords of an old classic—"Moonlight Serenade." The melody carried a weight of history, not just for Gertie, but for all of them. It was a song that seemed to connect the past and the present, a reminder of love, loss, and the power of memory.

Gertie hummed along; her eyes closed as the music transported her back to a night long ago. "Harold sang this to me on our wedding day," she whispered. "It still feels like yesterday."

Susan placed a hand on Gertie's shoulder, her heart full. "I'm glad you can remember it so clearly now. The trauma the first time on the machine was too much to bear, but as we continued talking to you, giving you the facts, you were able to fill in the blank spaces."

Gertie smiled. "Thanks to the two of you, it's like he's still here with me."

"Let's give the Birthday girl a good rendition of Happy Birthday." Mark winked at Gertie as everyone joined in.

When the voices of friends died down, Mark began singing a solo. His voice clear and warm and filled with love. He searched the crowd, his eyes landing on Susan.

"I want to dedicate that song to someone special," he said, his gaze never leaving Susan's. "To someone who taught me that the past, no matter how painful, can be a guide to a brighter future." His voice softened.

The crowd clapped, a murmur of agreement passing through them. Susan felt a lump rise in her throat as she made her way toward the stage, her heart heavy with both sadness and gratitude.

Mark set his guitar aside and pulled Susan onto the stage, her hands in his. "I don't think I would've made it here without you," he said quietly, his voice thick with emotion.

"You would've." Susan waved at the audience. "But I'm glad you didn't have to."

His thumb brushed over her knuckles. "I was afraid for so long—afraid of failing, afraid of opening up. But you…you made me believe in something again."

Tears shimmered in Susan's eyes as she whispered, "You did the same for me."

Without another word, Mark leaned in and kissed her—soft, tender, and full of the promise of their future. The crowd erupted in applause, but for them, the world had faded away, leaving only the two of them in that moment.

Susan smiled, resting her forehead against his. "Here's to us."

A word about the author…

S. A. Stolin is the pseudonym for an award-winning fiction author behind six gripping novels, a powerful non-fiction guide on overcoming childhood abuse, and short stories featured in Sherlock Holmes Mystery Magazine. S. A. began her career as an actress before transitioning into forensic psychology, where she gained deep insight into human behavior—an experience she now channels into crafting compelling, suspenseful stories. As a full-time writer, she loves to blend her diverse background into storytelling to keep readers on the edge of their seats.

When she's not weaving tales of intrigue, she loves traveling, cooking, and spending time with her husband, a retired physician. She enjoys hearing from readers and can be reached at sstolinsky24@gmail.com.

http://www.sastolinsky.com